WHEN THE RAIN STOPS

J S SUTTON

First published in Great Britain as a softback original in 2020

Copyright © J S Sutton

The moral right of this author has been asserted.

All characters and events in this publication, other than those clearly in the public domain, are fictitious and any resemblance to real persons, living or dead, is purely coincidental.

All rights reserved.

No part of this publication may be reproduced, stored in a retrieval system, or transmitted, in any form or by any means, without the prior permission in writing of the publisher, nor be otherwise circulated in any form of binding or cover other than that in which it is published and without a similar condition including this condition being imposed on the subsequent purchaser.

Typeset in Palatino

Design, typesetting and publishing by UK Book Publishing

www.ukbookpublishing.com

ISBN: 978-1-913179-76-2

For *Julie Woodward*, my number
one fan in heaven.

Author's Note: Although this book is amazing in its own right, it's best read while listening to *Synthwave music*.

PART 1:

Neon Playgrounds and Nuclear Wastelands

1

"When the rain stops it will be a miracle" thought David as he shut the bedroom curtains of his twenty third floor flat in the eastern block of New London known as Aurora Heights. The year is 2056 and Planet Earth has become uninhabitable due to climate change and thermo-nuclear war, so the Earth's residents live in a city in the clouds. Only criminals get sent to the Earth below to serve their prison sentences. He crosses the floor to switch the radio off before heading out to work. David Wright worked at the New London Metropolitan Police Station as a Detective Inspector and was working on a case involving the New London crime syndicate known as 'The New Krays'.

They started out as a group of youths who snatched purses and drank in front of small corner shops but as soon as they joined the big leagues, via a few shady deals with Neo Yuppies, they became quite formidable to the police department.

"Weather report," David said to his ocular fitbit as he locked his door and a box opened on the periphery of his vision. "Drag to centre!" he commanded. It read "Caution: Acid rain storm is imminent." Upon seeing this he sighed as he was already late for work and unlocked his door to retrieve his rubber trench coat and umbrella. David didn't mind the rain usually but acid rain was a different matter. Acid rain could seriously burn. He'd suffered an acid rain burn on his hand several years previously when he couldn't get to one of the many purpose built shelters dotted around the city in time. The doctor said he was lucky. David thought otherwise.

The bustling streets did nothing to improve David's already sour mood. People pushing past him, nearly knocking him over on several occasions. The neon signs burned into his eyes so every time he closed them against the brightness he could see a light purple outline of the building's logo for a good few minutes.

"You're joking, right?" exclaimed David as he sat across the desk from his boss in his office.

"Nope" said his boss Captain Lee, "you have to go to the surface, if anyone's gonna believe you're a hardened criminal enough to get in with the New

CHAPTER 1

Krays you have to do time, you've gotta make them think you've got dirt on you in order for them to trust you."

"But the surface, really?" pleaded David, furrowing his brow. "I can't go down there, I remember what it was like before the HMP colony, the weather was terrible, proper shit show."

"You'll hold that foul tongue in this office and you'll do as I say DI Wright!" bellowed Captain Lee.

"Fine," sighed David "what are my charges?"

"Homicide of another police officer" explained Captain Lee, a little calmer now.

It always slightly unnerved David how quickly Captain Lee's mood can change from jumping apeshit to euphoric calm, but that was Captain Lee.

David sat at his desk and sighed. "The surface?" He thought, "most of the people on the surface were put there by me, I'm gonna be really popular". He sipped his coffee and shuddered. Cold again, God who was making these coffees?

"How's it goin' cowboy?" a seductive voice said above him. "How come, out of all the officers in the building, you're the only one with a gun?" David smiled and looked up. DI Diane Saunders, brunette, standing 5 foot nothing and ten stone soaking wet.

"Because," David answered "out of all the

officers in the building I'm the only one who needs a gun". She smiled. She was pretty, even without make up she was pretty, but she wore it anyway. Much to her husband's disapproval. Controlling bastard. "She was a free spirit and he should nourish that" David thought.

"So" Diane continued "How long have they given you on the surface?"

"God, how do you know?" David said with a slight bit of embarrassment.

"Everybody knows" she said "it was suggested at last night's meeting."

"Yeah" David thought "I should really start turning up to those."

Six years. Six damn years on that Godforsaken rock. Just to get in with those wannabe hardmen. He threw his keys on the coffee table and sat down. "TV on!" he commanded wearily and the movie channel came on.

"Oh yes" he thought "I was watching this last night instead of being in the meeting" he laughed softly and ran his fingers through his hair. It's A Wonderful Life was on. Every time he saw this movie it made him think of his mother. He didn't know why.

When the movie finished, he had a shower and

CHAPTER 1

went to bed. He dreamed of Diane brushing her brunette hair and smiling before the alarm woke him up. Still raining. He showered and went to work. When he got there Captain Lee called him into his office.

"We need to move forward with the plan sooner than expected" he said "we can't really afford to lose time on this and since you find it so difficult to turn up to meetings I'll fill you in

on the details of the operation now."

Captain Lee scratched his temple. It was so obvious to David, and everyone else in the office for that matter, that Captain Lee had a wig.

"You'll get dropped just outside the town of Wrexham in North Wales by the site of HMP Berwyn. From there you'll find a way to Chester and rendezvous with an informant, they'll have more info for you."

That night, as it was the last night of freedom for a while, David was in New Soho to have a little fun. Neon lights advertising various uppers, downers and everything in between burned into his skull. He knew tomorrow morning he'd have to be up earlier than normal to have his ocular Fitbit removed and his old natural eye, the one he was born with, replaced. He wasn't looking forward to the procedure. But he knew that ocular Fitbit implants were a luxury and you can't have luxuries on the HMP colony. Plus it was a service issue for the purpose of crime solving. At least that's what he told the taxman. A hooker approached him as he came to a corner.

"Looking to party?" She asked. She was dressed like a punk from last century with purple hair and fishnets with a slight glint of heroine in her shallow eye sockets.

"Tell me," David said with a mischievous smile, "did you start turning tricks because you have a habit or the other way round?"

"Fuck you" she spat and walked away.

2

It was at the bar of the Neon Potato where David was sat. Alone and nursing a whiskey. "The last night of freedom" he slurred to a barman he thought was there, he couldn't really see. "For a while at least" he said into his glass as he took another sip. Over the music he heard a female voice.

"That's the fucker over there, by the bar!"

And at once he felt a sharp blow to the side of his head and the room spun then all of a sudden he saw the ceiling. A greasy looking Portuguese guy knelt over him and said "you don't wanna fuck my girl huh?" David was helped to his feet by hands he didn't know were there and said "sorry I don't do hookers, not humans anyway, gimme a lovely android anyday".

"You like androids?" The Portuguese guy asked "then I can help you."

"Alejandro" the female voice whined, and out stepped the purple haired punk from earlier, "what about me?"

Alejandro smiled and with one biomechanical fist bust David's nose.

"What the fuck!!!" David shouted as he cradled the blood already seeping from his nose.

"You should've just told her instead of being a dick" laughed Alejandro.

Hours later he barely stood in front of a grimy bathroom mirror. His bloodshot eyes slitted against the light. The android hooker walked from the bed in the dirty, dilapidated hotel room to join him.

"Wow!" She said, spaced out on whatever she took earlier "he busted your nose pretty bad".

"Lucky shot" David drunkenly grumbled.

"Whatever" she said "that'll be a hundred for the four hours". He crossed over to his rubber trench coat hanging on the back of a chair and got his wallet, paid her and collapsed on the bed as she left clumsily.

Later on the hologram of Captain Lee projected from the TV in the wall bellowed at David to wake up. He was late for his operation to replace his ocular Fitbit with his natural eye. He hated going to the doctor for anything let alone an operation. David rose from the bed, groaned and stumbled like the living dead then got ready to leave.

CHAPTER 2

At the back alley surgery David was sitting in the waiting room. There was no one else waiting so why was he? The receptionist sat on her arse on the phone to one of her friends. David thought she looked slightly Asian her hair was tied up that tight. He was on the verge of hangover sleep when the receptionist called out.

"David Wright? Dr Davies will see you now" he walked into the operating room and was greeted by a small Danny Devito looking guy with glasses.

"Ah Mr Wright, come in take a seat" he said with a near toothless grin "here for the ocular replacement surgery I hear". David sat on the recliner and with a stomp of the pedal by Dr Davies, was forced onto his back. Dr Davies then forced David's eye open with a steel clamp and said "you may feel a slight discomfort during the procedure."

"Yeah Doc" David thought "you're only ripping something out of my eye socket". Dr Davies then manoeuvred a machine that resembled a small version of the hook games you get at the arcade with a camera on top over his eye and proceeded to remove the ocular Fitbit. It felt like a dozen needles were being jammed in David's eye socket but he kept his cool. David gripped the arm rest to relieve the discomfort and gritted his teeth.

"Nearly over" Dr Davies said "keep still."

When he left the surgery David walked through the rain to the police station. He felt like he was in another world. He hated not having his ocular Fitbit but for his job he had to undergo the change. Suddenly, there arose an air raid siren from huge speakers mounted on top of the street lights. Acid rain was on its way. David rushed into one of the shelters to wait it out.

3

When the acid rain storm had passed David continued on his way to work. When he got there he sat at his desk and looked through his emails briefly before heading to the coffee room to see if Diane was working. There she stood, playing with her hair while waiting for the coffeemaker to finish.

"Hi" David said.

"Oh, hi" she replied quietly, she seemed preoccupied with something.

It was then that Bennet came in, he stank the place up so bad you could smell him before seeing him. Like a lingering bad smell that takes a while to wash out.

"Hi guys," he said to them both, cheerfully, "what's in the fridge today?" he opened the fridge and took out a sandwich filled with genetically modified meat and cheese.

"Is that yours?" David asked and smiled at

Diane, who smiled back but quickly went to seriousness when she realised Bennet was looking and didn't want to hurt his feelings any more than David already had.

David then turned back to Diane.

"You ok?" he asked.

"No" she replied "the police officer you're meant to kill to get you sent down is me".

"I would never do that" he said, reassuring her "but this is supposed to be a lie though right? Just so I have a story if I'm asked."

"I suppose" she replied "doesn't make the idea any easier to swallow."

Hours later, he was up before the judge for his sentencing. In 2056 the law system was quicker when it came to murder, especially when it came to a police officer murdering another police officer.

"You will serve a custodial sentence in the HMP colony on the surface for no longer than six years" the judge ordered "should you misbehave, your sentence will increase by four years per incident, so I suggest you keep your head down". From there David was taken to the underside of New London to be processed and sent down to the surface. He was stripped, searched, washed and put in his prison uniform. His head was shaved and he was given a tattoo with his prison number on his left forearm. All his belongings were archived until his release and he was taken to the pod bay to await transfer to the surface. When his pod came he was strapped in and the pod door closed.

Then the pod whirred to life and he was catapulted down a dark tunnel and ejected out into the sky. All he could see was orange and red dust and mist as he plummeted to the Earth's surface. With a crash he landed. The mist was especially pronounced here but he could slightly see the outline of the ruins of HMP Berwyn. The pod door opened and he was greeted with a rush of hot, thick air. He unstrapped himself and climbed out. The wind was gale forced and it took a few minutes for him to catch his breath. He looked about his surroundings. All he could see was a wasteland from the thermo-nuclear war. A stark contrast to New London, where there were neon lights and people pushing past one another. Now he just felt lonely.

He began the long trek to Chester to meet the informant. If he passed through Wrexham town he didn't notice. It was mostly obliterated by the nuclear warheads during the last skirmish. He trod on something and heard a metallic sound. Kneeling down he wiped away the dust and mud. It was a street sign. Warwick Avenue. He didn't realise he'd come this far, there were no buildings to indicate where he was. There was nothing but dust covered wasteland as far as he could see which was barely in front of him now the dust storm had kicked up.

He lifted a scarf he was given up in New London over his face and carried on walking.

He got to where he assumed Hope was. The dust storm had settled now and he could see the sky. He forgot how beautiful it was. He had a few seconds of splendour before New London obstructed his view by floating in the way. He had a twinge of jealousy as he looked up at the neon underbelly and thought of all the fun he could've had if he hadn't taken on this shit operation. He shook it off and carried on walking.

The informant was waiting for him on the banks of the river Dee. She was tall for a woman and supermodel slim with, what David assumed to be, blonde hair. She looked down her sunglasses at David as he approached and smiled.

"So you're David?" She asked.

"Yeah that's me" he replied "you the informant?"

"Tori" she replied pushing her sunglasses

back up her nose and reaching her hand out to be shaken. He reciprocated the motion and they touched for the first time. As they walked she explained that the New Krays weren't the only gang on the HMP colony but one of many.

Neo Yuppies couldn't really be called a gang on the HMP colony and generally kept their noses clean and would roll over on anyone if it meant they could shave off some years in their sentences. Up on New London their money made them somebody and could practically get away with most crimes. Down on the colony they were nobody.

Another gang were the Rough Housers. They were, before the war, a football firm who liked nothing more of a Saturday afternoon than to fight other firms. In New London they were generally frowned upon as what they lacked in brain power they more than made up for in muscle and numbers. This made them almost kings on the colony and David wasn't looking forward to meeting them.

The Off Gridders led a simple life but were weapons experts available to the highest bidder. They were country folk and farmers before the war so they knew their way around the wasteland better than most as they decided to stay on the surface to re-terraform the planet. They could be recognised by their knee high army boots and plaid shirts. David had never met an Off Gridder before so he was a little curious.

There were a few other gangs that roamed the colony but they were kept in check by the more prominent organisations and Tori didn't go into much detail about them.

4

All the gangs had their own compounds dotted around the city. Each one of them was run by a surface leader. A kind of Mafia Don if you will. But with all the power they're given, they had to answer to the Supreme Colony Boss who's compound stood on the site of, what was before the war, Chester Town Hall. She was cruel, cold hearted and callous but, if she liked you, she had the potential to be caring, fair and warm.

Tori took David straight to her to see what she thought of him. Everyone had to see the Supreme Colony Boss when they landed but David was a special exception as he was a cop killer.

When they arrived at the compound, they were stopped at the gates by security.

"Stop!" The guard ordered and Tori talked her way past him by flashing a bit of cleavage and stroking his face, whispering sweet nothings in his ear.

When it came time for David to pass, the guard put his giant hand on his chest and said "I don't know you."

"He's with me" Tori informed him.

"Sorry Tori" he said and he let David pass.

The compound was a hive of security and, as it was now dark, bathed in the light of spotlights mounted on towers made by bits of scrap metal doing a search sweep pattern.

"There's been a break in" Tori said as they walked towards the Supreme Colony Boss's tent.

"Who the hell would want to break in here?" David asked.

"Someone with a death wish" said Tori.

"Jesus" said David under his breath and almost feeling sorry for the poor son of a bitch when they found him. They got to the tent and entered via another security guard. The Supreme Colony Boss was standing with her back to them looking at a map on her table. She, noticing that they'd come in, slightly raised her hand for them to shut up and bare with her. When she was finished she turned to face them.

"My name is Lisa," she said "but everyone here calls me Boss and I expect you to do the same."

"Ok Boss" said David.

CHAPTER 4

"So," she asked "what brings you to the surface?"

"I killed a pig" David replied.

"May I ask why?" she asked, in an almost offended tone.

"Caught her in bed with my wife" David said, noticing in her eyes a sense of judgement already.

"HER?" she screamed, "You killed a female cop?"

David felt like a rabbit in headlights. The truck was careening towards him but he couldn't move.

"I don't fucking stand for violence against women," she said "whatever the circumstances. That's why I was put down here, I murdered my husband. Shot him point blank in the back of his head as he was watching TV. Self defence I call it. Fucker was beating me black and blue and, because he was a politician, he got away with it."

"I'm sorry," David said "I didn't know."

"Well now you do" she said.

"She doesn't like you" Tori said as they left the compound.

They walked in silence to the New Krays' compound and it gave David time to think.

Maybe he'd been too hastey, maybe he should've turned up to the meetings and picked out a male cop to supposedly kill. What the hell was he doing there?

When they got to the compound they were greeted by another security guard who let them pass with nothing more than a suspicious look and a nod of acknowledgement.

"The leader's tent is just ahead" Tori said as they passed through the compound, "shouldn't be too bad for ya in here, they hate cops and aren't too keen on females either."

"So they're gay?" David asked.

"No. Misogynistic"

"But you said-"

"Look" Tori turned around, "they're not gay they just don't have any respect for women, they believe women should just cook and clean after them. The Supreme Colony Boss doesn't care much for the New Krays and they don't care much for her, they only keep a truce to uphold order, prevent riots and stuff like that."

"Upholding order? This is a prison colony for fuck sake" David thought and they carried on walking.

They got to the tent just as a snow storm began. Since the war the weather everywhere had been all four seasons in one day and if you weren't careful you could get caught out in a cluster storm, all four seasons at once. People up on New London only had rain and acid rain to compete with. They were the lucky ones. The leader was sat on a scrap metal throne, stroking the head of a scantily clad woman who was kneeling at his side. He smiled as David and Tori entered.

"So you're the new guy?" He said and his smile got wider. It was at this point David noticed the leader barely had any teeth.

"Y-yeah" David answered, trying his best 'I'm afraid of you' stutter. Tori had told him that the leader liked people who feared him, some sort of God complex she guessed.

"What brings ya down here?" The leader said with a thick Irish accent.

"He's a cop killer" Tori answered for him.

"Cop killer?" The leader repeated, one eyebrow raised in surprise.

"Caught her in bed with my wife" David repeated the lie.

"Don't blame ya for killing her then" the leader said "I'm Patrick but you can call me Paddy, by what name am I honoured to address thee?"

"David."

"Well David," Paddy said, rising from his scrap

metal throne "you're among friends now, but in order to get in with us proper," he lifts his belt up to his stomach as it was falling, "you must do me a solid favour."

"Anything" said David.

"Good," Paddy said with a satisfactory smile, "I've got a shipment coming in from Calais to Dover and I want you to collect it, you can take Tori with you for backup should you need it, she's quite handy for a woman."

Hours later they were on the road in a jeep with Tori at the wheel.

"What's this shipment then?" asked David.

"Its a batch of guns Paddy bought from the French not long ago," Tori replied, "they're usually trustworthy so don't expect anything to go off, as long as you don't go off, you don't harbour any deep seated hatred for our cousins over yonder sea do you?"

"Nope I'm fine with the French."

"Good. Did you notice Paddy hardly had any teeth?"

"Yeah."

"That's what poor personal hygiene and trying to be gang leader gets you" Tori smiled at David.

When they got to the docks at Dover they

CHAPTER 4

parked the jeep and got out. The French were already there with several crates filled with guns.

"What does Paddy need all these guns for?" asked David.

"He's secretly planning war on the Supreme Colony Boss for dominance of the colony" Tori replied.

They walked up to the meeting spot and greeted the French.

"We have the goods" the interpreter said "you got the payment?"

Tori took a card from her back pocket and handed it to them.

"You and the goods stay put while we check this" the interpreter ordered.

One of the French took a chip card device from his satchel and scanned the card through.

"Ok," the interpreter said "it's all there, pleasure doing business with you, have a nice day."

He smiled and both parties left.

"So," David began as they put the crates in the jeep, "why would Paddy want war on the Boss and furthermore why would the French help him?"

"Well" replied Tori "Paddy hates having to answer to a woman and if anyone hates her more than him it's the French and for the same reason."

They put the last crate in the back of the jeep and got in. The engine roared to life and they sped off. When they got to where Birmingham used to be, Tori stopped the jeep and, in no time at all, her hands were on him, unbuttoning his trousers. She climbed over and they made love right there on the side of the road.

5

Afterwards, the sun rose over the desolate fields of dust and mud. Chester was quiet and still. Nobody was awake save for the day guards of the various compounds that dotted what was left of the city following the war and collapse of society. David was dumbfounded that Tori would do what she did, bearing in mind that they had just met really and he liked androids not humans, but he wasn't complaining either way. When they got back to the New Krays' compound they went to sleep. He dreamed of Diane, Captain Lee, Alejandro, the barman he barely saw at the Neon Potato….

She shook him awake at nightfall. He was sweating profusely. They got up and dressed then went to see Paddy to find out if there were any more jobs that needed doing.

On their way to the tent they were stopped by a group of men.

"Ah shit" Tori said under her breath.

It was Ricky and his brothers John and Georgey-boy.

"Hey Tori" Ricky sang, smiling from ear to ear, he was high on something smuggled down from New London.

"Hi Ricky" Tori said, wearly.

"This your new fella?" Ricky pointed at David.

"This is the new guy."

"Ain't no difference to you eh Tori?" laughed Georgey-boy.

"What's that supposed to mean?" Tori said, a little offended by the remark.

"Just you have a knack for layin' the newbies is all" said John.

David started to get annoyed, who the hell were these guys?

"Looks like your man is getting heated" Ricky said.

"No he's fine" Tori said, protectively.

"I can look after myself" David protested.

"See?" Georgey-boy said, "he can look after himself."

"David" Tori took his arm "you don't have to do this."

David began to say he was fine when Ricky's fist flew through the air and struck his cheek. David hit the ground with a thump and Ricky advanced on him. David shot to his feet and landed a good punch on Ricky's nose, knocking the man off his feet. John and Georgey-boy began to make their move but stopped when Paddy shot up between them.

"Hazing the new guy eh?" Paddy said.

The two thugs backed away and looked at their feet sheepishly.

"Just getting acquainted." Ricky said from the floor, cradling his nose.

Paddy turned to David.

"A word."

"Sure."

When they got to the tent another storm whipped up.

"I suppose" Paddy began as he sat on his throne, "you're wondering why I don't have many teeth. It's because of men like Ricky and his brothers. I'd be very careful if I were you. You're gonna have a wee bit of bother off them when I'm not around. Mark my words, they don't let things go."

David nodded in acknowledgement of the sage advice.

"So you want another job?" Paddy said.

"If there is any" Tori answered, still a bit

flustered from the incident outside.

"Well" Paddy began as he started stroking the head of his woman, it was a different one this time, a redhead, "there's an individual, owes me a couple thou, I want you," he points at David and Tori "to go collect it."

"Where will we find them?" asked David.

"He lives in the Snowdonia Mountain Range in a hut, don't be too rough with him, he's a valuable asset."

"Ok."

"I like a man who doesn't ask many questions" Paddy grinned and exposed what little teeth he had left, David thought he was going to be sick, "just a get up and go kinda man, asks enough to know what he's doing then," Paddy made a gesture with his hand to signify something exploding in smoke, "gone."

As they made their way to the jeep, Tori grabbed a hold of David and kissed him passionately. He pushed her away and said "sorry, I like androids."

The look of disappointment on her face almost killed him with guilt.

"We need to focus on the task at hand and not get distracted by our feelings."

"Ok" she said glumly and carried on walking to

CHAPTER 5

the jeep.

The journey to Snowdonia passed in relative, awkward silence. The tension was killing David as every time he went to speak, Tori shot him an angry glance as if to say "shut the fuck up."

They arrived at the foot of Mount Snowdon where the hut was and were greeted by the individual that owed Paddy the money. He was a big guy. David was wondering how they were expected to rough this guy up even slightly.

"You here for the money?" His gruff voice reverberated in David's ears.

"Yeah," David said "Paddy says we gotta rough you up a bit." The big guy smiled.

"Come in first," he said "grant me a cup of tea before you 'rough me up'." His smile widened at the thought of this scrawny guy and this skirt trying their luck.

"Come in" the individual said "you can have something to eat."

"Let me just stop you there," Tori said "we're here for the money, that's all."

They entered the hut and surveyed the place in case there was anyone else there who could jump out. The fire in the corner was flickering upwards and warmed the place nicely, although David wondered how this guy was able to get firewood seeing as though all plant life was eradicated during the last years of the war.

The individual noticed David looking at the fire and smiled.

"It's electric," he said "powered by the generator outside, in the back, a bit funny when it's cold but works nicely other times."

The individual lightly pushed past David and walked to a kitchen area in the opposite corner to the fire. He began preparing the tea and David wondered if he knew what was about to happen.

6

He staggered out the door, blood soaked and tired. The light burned his eyes and he struggled to breathe. The stab wound in his side was weeping profusely and he cradled it as he stumbled on the uneven ground. David needed to get to a doctor quickly or he'll die. He got to the jeep, opened the driver side door and climbed in. He took a moment to steady himself then started the engine. It was a tough night that he'd rather forget, but that was impossible.

The individual introduced himself as Bruno. He used to be a bodybuilder back before the war and David and Tori could definitely see he wasn't lying. He was huge, how did he maintain that shape? He was all alone out here with nothing for company except the odd care package that was sent from the compounds in Chester and the loans that he received from Paddy. And furthermore what did he need the money for? He was completely self sufficient with a generator out the back and a genetically modified vegetable garden in the front, 'cash

   hoarder probably' David thought.

   "Please, sit." He gestured to a tattered 3 piece suite in front of the fire then carried on preparing his meal.

   "Are you hungry?" He asked, David and Tori shook their heads in unison, "you really should eat something," he suggested "it's a long way back to Chester."

   Once the meal was ready and cooked, they all sat in front of the fire.

   "A man sure does get lonely out here," Bruno said, "kinda makes you crazy."

   He smiled at Tori, leared at her really. David started to feel empathetically uncomfortable for Tori. He didn't like the way Bruno was looking at her, like a predator scoping its prey. But he guessed she might be used to it, being one of the only women in the colony and Bruno being so far from everyone else. If Bruno wanted to do something to Tori David couldn't stop him, not really, but he'd try.

   "I know why you won't eat," Bruno said, a little paranoid now, "you think just because I owe Paddy

I won't pay up and try to poison you."

"No!" They both said, again in unison.

Bruno set his plate down and started to cry.

"Nobody who comes here wants my food," he said, between sobs, "it's like they think I'm a psycho killer or something, just because I bludgeoned my wife to death for sleeping with the postman in my own fucking bed!!!" He started to hyperventilate between half screams and whimpers, "I mean," he pointed to David, "wouldn't you do that?"

He paused for David's reply and, when it took David a few seconds to figure out it wasn't a rhetorical question, he began to stare angrily. Bruno stood, his mood beginning to change slightly, and took his plate to the kitchen.

David and Tori exchanged glances of surprise and a little fear. Bruno began rooting through the draws like he was looking for something, found it then shut draws with a loud clanging sound. He then stood behind them and exclaimed "I'm so lonely!" David and Tori felt a knock to the head and all went black.

7

"Wakey, wakey" Bruno sang and David tried opening his eyes. They were so heavy.

"This'll wake ya" Bruno assured and jammed a knife into David's side and twisted it. David's eyes opened with a start and he screamed out in pain. Everything had a reddish tint and he realized he was bleeding from the head, more specifically where he'd been hit. He tried to move but couldn't. He stared down at his hands and saw they were bound to a chair with rope.

"LEAVE HIM ALONE!!" Screamed Tori from the corner. She was in a cage and, like David, was bleeding from the head.

David looked, a little confused, over to Bruno who stood naked and laughing at Tori's cries of pain. She was begging to be let out, that they can just go and forget the money. Bruno had none of it. There was something he wanted though, David and

CHAPTER 7

Tori could see it in his eyes.

"No," said David, pleading as Bruno sauntered over to Tori's cage, "no!"

Bruno stopped and, looking over at David, smiled crazily. He continued this expression as he carried on walking to the cage. He unlocked the cage and opened the door.

"No!" David screamed as he rocked the chair from side to side, trying to escape. Tori shrank back from Bruno's outstretched hand and he grabbed her ankle, pulled her out kicking and screaming and started to undress her forcibly. She resisted so he grabbed a hammer and struck her again and again until she stopped moving. David stared in horror at what he was witnessing, begging Bruno to stop. It was then, with a leering, taunting smile at David, Bruno began to rape Tori's unconscious body. David began to weep with sorrow and frustration, he rocked from side to side trying to escape, trying to end this horrific scene. He couldn't. The ropes were too tight.

When Bruno finished, he stood and breathed deep from the forceful exertions and, looking sideways at David, smiled.

David never felt as much hatred as he did now, looking through tears of anger and sadness he resolved to kill this bastard. Even if it killed him too, he was going to kill Bruno.

"She's filthy," Bruno mumbled, "I'm going to take a bath."

When Bruno left, David began to struggle in the chair again and to his delight the rope started to give. Within minutes of hard struggle the rope finally gave way and David was free. He creeped over to Tori's ragdoll body and tried to wake her. Nothing. He felt for her pulse. Nothing. He'd killed her. He'd actually killed her. He heard Bruno singing in the bathroom as he washed and felt the anger rise up his throat like water in a bubbling pan. Quietly he picked up a piece of rope and creeped to the bathroom.

"Washing the filthy bitch off me" Bruno was singing as David creeped up on him and, quickly wrapping the rope around his neck, choked the fucking life out of him. For extra effect, David pushed Bruno under the water and tightened the rope until the bubbles stopped.

When he was sure Bruno was dead, David limped over to Tori's lifeless body. The adrenaline rush quickly subsiding, he felt the pain in his side from his stab wound creep up on him. He lay down next to Tori's body and wept a while. He didn't

CHAPTER 7

love her in the way she'd wanted but it still hurt him to witness her last moments, her last aching whimper as Bruno brought the hammer down on her head. He wanted to know why. Why had Bruno done this? It couldn't have been loneliness or mental illness. He resolved to get up and find out. He struggled to his feet and walked into the bedroom, searched the draws and the closet, under the bed and in the pillow case until he found it. A newspaper clipping of David holding what looked like a certificate, shaking hands with Captain Lee and smiling. That's it. David remembered now. Bruno was his last case before he took the New Krays case. The man who murdered who he thought to be his cheating wife but who turned out to be just a random woman. Bruno had known David was a cop. He could have told Paddy and the rest if David hadn't had killed him. His cover would have been blown and he would have been as dead as Bruno was now. Drowned and strangled in a dirty bathtub.

8

David looked up from the steering wheel. He saw Captain Lee smiling and waving at him in the middle of the road.

"What the fuck?" He said under his breath. He was bleeding heavily and needed to get back to the compound fast. He was in where he believed Saltney was so he wasn't far. Suddenly, as if his day couldn't get any worse, the engine cut out. No fuel and no way of jump starting the battery. He got out and stumbled over into the roadside. Using every ounce of strength in him he stood up and fell against the jeep, steadied himself and started walking.

He got to the banks of the river Dee and collapsed.

All of a sudden he was back in New London and it was raining as per usual. He was wearing his rubber trench coat and he had hair again. He checked his forearm, no prison number tattoo. He

CHAPTER 8

looked around at his surroundings. He was at a crime scene that was strangely familiar. A back alley barely illuminated by neon and siren lights, flashing blue and red and reflecting in the puddles. It was night time. Head propped up against a dumpster, lay a body, barely noticeable face as the blood stained most of it and the hair was parted in the middle by an opening made by a probable heavy, blunt object. From the rest of the body he could see it was a woman.

"Lydia Walton." A voice said and David looked around to see where it came from. It sounded like Diane but he wasn't sure. He knelt by the body and inspected it, searching for clues as to what exactly happened here. He rooted through his pockets for some latex gloves, found them and put them on all the while he didn't take his eyes off the body.

"We need to move the body, before any evidence is swept away by the rain," he ordered "where's the coroner?"

"He's on his way" the voice that could be Diane said "he's been to a charity gala uptown."

"Oh how nice" David said dryly under his breath.

As he stood, he ordered someone to zip the body up to preserve the evidence and took the gloves off, putting them in his pocket. He looked around and saw he was completely alone in the alley.

"What the fuck is this Stanley Kubrick movie shit?" He said out loud. He looked down at his feet. No body. He looked up again and saw there was still the neon and the siren lights. Flashing, still flashing.

"David?" He heard a voice from the end of the alley. Confused, he walked to where it came from and looked left and right. Nothing but empty streets. No people, no cars, but there were still flashing lights.

"David, come back David!" The voice ordered. Suddenly he was pulled upwards to a light in the sky, it morphed into circles in a hexagonal arrangement and he felt a sharp slap to his left cheek. Blinking rapidly, he shook his head and tried to sit up. He felt a sharp pain where Bruno had stabbed him and winced. He lay back down and tried to relax.

"Where am I?" He asked a seemingly empty room.

"Off-gridder's complex," a voice replied "medical bay."

His throat was dry so he swallowed before speaking again.

CHAPTER 8

"How'd you know my name?" He asked.

"Well," the voice began, "we have a database of all new inmates that come down here from the processing centre on New London, we ran your prison number through our computers and your name came up. David Wright. DI David Wright."

His eyes shot open and he sat up quickly, banging his head on the light and ignoring the pain in his side. When his eyes adjusted to the light he was greeted by a tall man in surgeon's uniform and the boss, who stood against the door frame with a pair of mirror shades on, both were staring at him.

"So now," the boss said, she moved away from the door and started towards him, "we know who you are, but, what we don't know, is why you're here."

David began to search his brain for a lie and found one.

"I told you," he began "I killed a cop."

The boss stopped a few feet away and smiled.

"So you say," she turned away from him and continued, "but I don't believe you, you see many different types of people come and go in these parts, I've met nearly every one of them, and I like to think I'm a good judge of character, however, you fascinate me David, I've never been proven wrong

41

in my assumptions before now, that doesn't mean I like you, I just find you useful."

David was puzzled by this remark and went to enquire but thought better of it and remained silent.

She turned round and continued.

"I want you to spy for me on the New Krays."

David looked over at the man in surgeon's uniform who remained quiet throughout the entire conversation. He was smiling beneath his face mask.

"Who's this?" David asked.

"This," she replied and walked over to the man in surgeon's uniform and placed a hand on his shoulder, "is the man that discovered you on the banks of the Dee and saved your life, doctor Ira."

"Pleased to meet you properly David," said Dr. Ira, in a surprisingly high voice for a man of his height, David struggled to differentiate between the boss and the doctor.

"Now that introductions are out of the way," the boss interjected "we still have the business of you spying for me."

"Say I do," David began, "what do I get?"

"The man drives a hard bargain," the boss said, looked over at Dr Ira and laughed, "you get impunity from all incidents out of your control and

CHAPTER 8

I keep your secret from Paddy and his boys."

David considered this briefly.

"Sounds fair" he said.

The boss turned away to leave but stopped.

"Why isn't Tori with you?" She asked.

David told her everything and when he was finished she wiped a tear from her cheek and left.

PART 2:

Double Agent Wright

9

It was a rainy night when David returned to the New Krays' compound. He contemplated the offer from the boss and his answer. Was he being more deceitful than he already had been? He couldn't decide. He went straight to see Paddy to report what had happened in the hut at the slopes of Snowdonia.

"There was nothing you could do?" Asked Paddy.

"No," David said "I was bound to the chair by rope, but when I was free I used that rope to choke the fucker in the tub."

"I know I said don't rough him up but you had no choice given the circumstances my boy" said Paddy.

"I just wish Tori was still alive" said Paddy's pet woman.

Paddy raised his hand to the woman, who flinched, then lowered it saying "I share your sentiment but please, kindly shut the fuck up."

A guard ran into the tent.

"Sir," he said, between breaths, "David has a visitor from above. Name of Diane."

David's heart leaped in his throat. She was supposed to be dead, according to the people down here, how will he squirm his way out of this one? What lie could he conjure to ensure his safety?

When Diane entered the tent she ran to David and gave him a passionate kiss on his lips.

"Baby!" She exclaimed "I missed you."

"You know," Paddy said, pointing behind him with his thumb, "there's a tent for that sort of thing in the back, please feel free."

"Thanks" David said, grinning.

When they got to the tent they sat on the camping bed side by side. David told Diane everything that had happened so far since he'd been down here. When he finished she looked concerned.

"I get the feeling," she said "he's gonna ask you to spy on the boss, if he does then do it, you can't afford to lose face with these guys and you can't afford to lose trust with the boss. Here," she reaches into her satchel and pulls out a flare gun, "when the battle starts, fire this into the sky and someone will

CHAPTER 9

see and send a drone to pick you up. Meanwhile I'll smooth things over with Captain Lee and the judge and get you an early release for good behaviour."

"Thanks," he said "I really appreciate this."

He took the flare gun and hid it in his prison uniform pocket.

When she left, Paddy called David into his tent.

"I want you to spy on the boss" he said, just like Diane had predicted.

"Ok," said David "what do I need to know?"

Paddy smiled his usual toothless grin.

"She's not a woman of particular habits, that we know of anyhow," Paddy said "she mainly stays in her compound. What we do know is that she's got a map of the city and contacts with New London, she's in charge of what and who comes and goes to the colony."

"What do you need me to do?" Asked David.

"I need that map and her black book of contacts so I can get in on her action," Paddy replied "do this and I'll make a call to the New Krays up on New London and get a nice, shiny recommendation so you have a paid position when you leave us."

"Nice," David said "thank you."

"No problem," Paddy said "tell her you're not happy with us and would like to join her group for awhile to see if it's any better. Then once you've gained her trust simply take the map and the little black book and come back."

Some time later, David was in the boss's compound again. He told her what Paddy was planning to do.

"Does he now?" she said, grinning, "well he can have the map no problem, i'll just have another one printed up, but he can fuck off if he thinks he's having my little black book."

"You don't understand," David began, "if I show up with just the map he's gonna-"

"It's you who doesn't understand," she interrupted, " what situation you're in David."

He looked at his shoes and shuffled them a bit, defeated by her threat.

"Thought so," she said, turning to her bodyguard who stood in the corner and smiled, "you see, I run shit down here, what I want done, gets done and I won't take shit off anyone, let alone a cop killer like you, a WOMAN cop killer to boot. You can go now Miles," she said to her bodyguard "I wanna chat to David alone." Miles left, not looking too happy about it but he took orders from her, and only her.

"We both know what's going on here," she

CHAPTER 9

began, when Miles left, "so I'll cut you a deal. You go to the off-gridders and retrieve something for me and I'll give you a pat on the head and the little black book. I own two in case one of them was stolen, Paddy can have the old one and I keep the new one and call every number to tell them not to do business with him, he's not having a slice of my pie."

"What do you need?" David asked.

"I can see why Paddy likes you," she laughed, "I need a crate of guns, if Paddy wants a war he's got one, I'll send Miles with you as back up, in case anything happens, just make sure you don't lose him like you lost Tori."

That last comment cut David like a knife.

He wiped a tear away when she dismissed him from the meeting. She didn't have to bring up Tori, and that made him sick.

"Bitch," he said under his breath as he left "she didn't need to say that."

His mood was alleviated when he found, waiting for him in a dusty suitcase that reeked of age, overuse and something fishy that David didn't even want to know, the map he needed for Paddy, all he needed now was that black book.

"We goin to the off-gridders huh?" said Miles,

enthusiastically.

"Yeah we're going to the off-gridders." said David, weary and downtrodden, like a parent who confirms for the zillionth time that they're going to disney world (which was obliterated in the fourth nuclear attack on American soil.)

He turned to Miles and said "where exactly do these off-gridders live?"

"On the outskirts of the city there are a few outposts they call home, they wanna be free with nature whatever that means these days, there's no nature to be free with except the bugs, and they've mutated exponentially."

"Mutants?" David asked, a little annoyed with Tori, or anyone else for that matter, for not telling him.

They got to the head outpost somewhere near where the greyhound park was in what felt like no time at all. There they met a tubby guy named Teddy who offered to show them to the pick up point for the weapons.

All the way there he was talking non stop about his damned cattle and how they'd be mating soon, David feigned interest. When they finally got to the pick up point somewhere where Blacon used to be he, telling them to wait, left to go get the rest of the

CHAPTER 9

boys.

As they waited there began a buzzing sound and David noticed Miles becoming uneasy.

"What's the matter? Be cool" he said.

"I can't," Miles said "I know what's coming."

"What?"

"Mutated wasps."

Suddenly the buzzing sound got closer and they both looked towards where it came from.

10

David didn't mind wasps usually. He left them alone and they left him alone. He remembered one summer, before the war, when he went to Bala Lake with his grandparents. They rented a nice, huge, three berth caravan for the summer. He was twelve at the time. He met a girl and they fell in summer love. The kind of love that only survives the week or so that they were there, her with her freckles, black hair and braces, him with his pre-braces buckteeth and milk bottle glasses, but to them it was for all eternity. One day they were by the stream, canoodling as young lovers do, when a wasp landed on her forearm. She began to freak out.

"I hate wasps!!! I hate 'em I hate 'em I HATE 'EM!!!!!"

"Don't worry," he reassured her, "they'll leave you alone if you leave them alone."

Gently he brushed it off and kissed her as

passionately as her braces would allow.

A few days later, she was out of his life, gone, back home to live the rest of her life, probably met a boy, got married and had kids. But he never forgot that summer.

Miles shook David out of his stupor as the buzzing got louder and louder like a crescendo of didgeridoos. Then they saw the wasps. Slightly bigger than house cats they came, stingers at the ready. David broke his fear and wonder to look for heavy, blunt objects they could use to defend themselves. Nothing to hand.

"Shiiit" he said.

"Tell me about it" Miles replied, shaking uncontrollably.

Suddenly David saw a fence consisting of two planks of wood connected by a thin streak of barbed wire. He ran and pulled them out of the ground and passed one to Miles.

Together they prepared for battle. All of a sudden they heard a sound like something thin and metal being shot through the air at the speed of knots. Then there came a pink ray of some kind and the lead wasp exploded. The rest of the wasps changed course and started for the sound, more sounds and pink rays then the wasps were no more.

"Did you see that?" asked a voice to the left of them.

David and Miles looked towards the voice and they were met with a gang of rough looking people. One of them was holding a triple barreled rifle but handed it over to one of his cronies before he continued.

"That's the capability of your purchase gentlemen, impressed?"

David and Miles both nodded in unified agreement.

The man who had the rifle, who David assumed to be the leader, stepped forward and said

"do you have the money?"

"Yes" Miles replied, and dug into his pockets for the credit chip the boss had given him previously.

The transaction took place and David and Miles both turned to leave but the leader stopped them.

"Stay," he pleaded "hang out with us, we have beer, wine, women, meat, maybe a bed for the night?"

David was unsure but Miles was easily swayed.

"How are we meant to get these to the boss?" David asked.

"We'll send for someone tomorrow," Miles said at the side of his mouth "I haven't had fun in a

CHAPTER 10

while."

Hours later they were sat around a campfire, sipping wine and eating a plate of genetically modified meat and vegetables. Each had a woman on their arm although David felt uncomfortable. He'd asked earlier if they had any android women but there were none on the colony so he'd have to make do with human women. It was something about the touch of synthetic skin that did it for David, he couldn't explain why. Maybe because androids were programmed to enjoy sex that made David feel unthreatened, secure in the idea that they would enjoy sex with him and not ever make him feel inadiquet in that department. Though he hadn't had any complaints from past human relationships, he still felt insecure due to his first ever tryst with a human girl. He was seventeen and at a party when he met her. They talked and drank most of the night. When the wee small hours came they were in bed together. He was nervous, she was not as this wasn't her first time with a boy. He thought she'd be gentle, kind and respectful, understanding that this was his first time and he wouldn't be good at it. But she wasn't. Five minutes later she was getting dressed laughing. He felt embarrassed, degraded and useless. How dare she, he thought. When he got back to his parents house later on, he crept in and slept on the sofa. He was woken by his father an hour later when he lugged a box through the front door.

"Here's something I bought for us, now your mother's gone" he said to David.

He unboxed something that would change David's life forever.

An android maid.

She cooked, cleaned, read to David's little sister Tilda at bedtime.

She was also quite beautiful, David thought.

She had dark hair, green eyes and a figure that would put any super model to shame. Her name was Traci.

One day, when David came back from college, his parents weren't home and it was just him and Traci. She was cooking his favorite meal and noticed David was staring at her. He couldn't help it, she was stunning. Her smile brightened his day and never failed to get a smile back from him. She turned to him and stopped cooking.

"Hello David," she said "how was college today?"

"Tough," he said, "had an exam, did well I think."

CHAPTER 10

"Good," she replied and turned to carry on cooking.

He approached her and ventured in for a kiss.

She turned and reciprocated the action, kissing him passionately.

Turning the cooker off, they both went up to his room.

There, in the light of the sun through his blinds, they made love and it was a much better experience than his first time. She was kind, loving and never made him feel insecure about any of it.

The touch of her rubberised, plastic skin made him shudder with delight and lust. She was gentle, her kisses covered his body. She was programmed to know what she was doing but she didn't take full control.

An hour later, as they were both laying, sweaty and satisfied, his parents came home and they rushed to dress. They never spoke of the encounter again but it was imprinted on David's psyche for life. He forever searched for another Traci.

11

The morning after, David woke up earlier than Miles and watched the sun rise. The storm of the night had passed and the sun shone red in its early light. It was time to leave the outpost and return to the boss's compound with the merchandise. When the sun reached its morning peak he woke Miles and they drove home in a jeep the off-gridders lent them with the crates in the back.

When they returned and the boss was happy with the guns, she gave him the book and David decided to go back to the New Kray's compound and report to Paddy.

Paddy had a different pet woman this time, a blonde with big breasts, and like always he was stroking her head as he pondered what David had told him.

"I mean," David said "these guns are top of the line, it'll be hard to defeat her with what she's got

CHAPTER 11

now."

"But," Paddy said, tapping the front cover of the little black book which teetered on the arm of his corrugated iron throne "now I have the book I can just call up her contacts and-"

"She said she's gonna call up all her contacts and tell them not to do business with you" David interrupted.

"WHAT!!" Paddy screamed as he quickly got to his feet, his pet woman flinched.

"I'm sorry," David said "that's just what she told me."

"Well a fat lot of good this book is to me."

"What should I do?"

"Go, no, creep back to the compound and get her second copy, then we'll talk about that nice shiny recommendation."

"Ok."

"Choose from our selection of guns in the back, going in hard or quiet?"

"Quiet would be best, but i'll need something loud and powerful if i'm spotted."

"Go on then" Paddy said, gesturing behind him.

David browsed the selection of guns before him before picking up a 9mm beretta with a silencer and an AK47 for if he's spotted creeping into the boss's territory, he'd be hunted down and shot.

Next he picked the ammunition, the beretta had quite a few rounds in it already but there's a chance he'd need more so he packed an extra clip in case. Same deal with the AK but he's guessing he needs more than a few clips for that, just to be on the safe side.

Once he was tooled up and ready to go, he reported back to Paddy to go over the map for any way of getting in without being noticed. It was at this point he remembered what Tori said.

"Somebody tried breaking in."

He remembered searchlights and didn't they have dogs?

Either way there was talk of them crucifying him and leaving the body for the birds. There were no more birds so that part was fabricated.

He put his doubts to the back of his mind (cop training came useful sometimes) and returned to study the map with Paddy.

Now there were a pile of boxes, food, ammunition, essential items etc, stacked up by one of the guard's towers in the south east of the building. He could get up there, take out the guard and climb down the ladder. After that he'd have to stay in the shade of a few tents til he got to the

CHAPTER 11

boss's tent. After that he should creep inside, take the book and, using the same way he came in, get out.

"Sounds easy enough," David said "but this map doesn't show the other guard's patrol path. I've seen it, one of them walks from north west to south west but he doesn't go behind the tents so I may not be in the shade for long, another guy goes the same route but the other side. The rest are either in the middle or on the other guard towers."

"Well," Paddy said, standing up "you do that and I'll get on the blower to New London people and get you that recommendation."

When David got to the boss's compound he crept to the boxes stacked up next to the wall, climbed up with ease and took out the guard with the silenced beretta. Searching him, he found a sniper model of the triple barreled rifle he'd bought from the off-gridders earlier.

He descended the ladder and made his way behind the tents, stopping every moment or so to watch for the guards. When he finally got to the boss's tent he stopped, he could hear voices coming from inside. Ricky's voice.

"We're not happy with Paddy, gone soft, always choosing that new guy David to do all his jobs, we want recognition for what we do too."

"Yeah," said another voice, Georgey-boy, "and that David twat killed our Tori."

"Sounds to me," the boss "like your problem isn't with Paddy, but this new guy."

"Either way we wanna join you lot" Ricky said.

"We're over capacity at the moment but we'll let you know if anything comes up" said the boss.

She called in Miles who escorted the men out of the tent and all went quiet.

David crawled under the tent and saw that it was empty. The boss was somewhere in the compound. He took the opportunity to lay waste by looking everywhere for the little black book.

Some moments later, he searched the underside of the bed and found it just as he heard noises outside. He grabbed the book and stood up sharply then, with haste, he crawled out where he came in and hid.

"WHERE IS IT?!!! She screamed as David started to make his move behind the other tents. He had to get out now. "Quickly" he said to himself under his breath. As he got to the ladder that would take him back up to the guard tower and over the wall to freedom, there was a guard having a smoke right at the foot of the ladder. Quickly, quietly

CHAPTER 11

and with efficiency, he dispatched the guard with his silenced beretta and climbed up the ladder, holstering his gun in the process.

He turned to the compound as he got to the top of the ladder and saw the boss leaving her tent in a huff.

"One of those New Krays twats has my book I know it, send word to the other compounds, Ricky and Georgey-boy DEAD!!!"

"Yes boss" a guard said and walked off.

David couldn't help laughing as he climbed down the boxes and ran for his life back to the New Krays's compound.

Upon his return Paddy greeted him with a smile.

"Well sonny boy," he said to David "you got the job, you should be hearing from them in a few weeks."

"Thank you" David replied.

"Did you get the book? Paddy hopefully and excitedly inquired.

"I got the book," David said, handing him the book "and I got this beauty too."

He handed Paddy the triple barrelled sniper rifle.

"We may not have stood a chance before but we

do now slightly" he said as Paddy inspected the gun with a huge cheshire cat grin on his face.

Suddenly a guard burst through the tents opening.

"Sir!" he said panting "the boss, she's outside with all her boys!! Complaining that one of your boys took something of great value to her."

Paddy looked at David.

"I was quiet enough" he said and Paddy nodded in belief.

"But Ricky and Georgey-boy were there, wanting to join them" David said.

Paddy had a look on his face that signified betrayal and hurt.

"Looks to me," Paddy said, sighing "that the war has begun, I'll deal with those two later."

12

The New Krays didn't take long to gear up for battle. The boss and her men were tooled up to the teeth, ready for a showdown. Paddy's pet women were herded underground for protection. Paddy approached the gates and the boss did the same. Then the rain started as they spoke.

"You," she began "have something of mine, something I'd like back."

"You mean this?" Paddy said, holding up the book and smiling.

"Yes, that."

"Well you can't have it back, it belongs to me now."

"You have five seconds to give me what's mine or I blow this place to holy hell."

"Like I care."

"Fine."

She walked back to her men and commanded "on my order men!" and they aimed their rifles at the compound. The New Krays did also and a standoff began.

"FIRE!!" Paddy and the boss shouted in unison and hell broke loose in a flurry of pink rays
and bullets.

David, remembering the plan, ran to the top of a guard tower and fired the flare gun to the sky. In no time at all a police drone came sweeping down and David grabbed hold of its protruding metal arm. Flying upwards, he looked down at the carnage.

He saw Paddy hiding behind a wall shooting. Paddy looked up, saw David flying away and shouted "DAAAVIIIDD!!!" before being bisected by a pink ray.

"Goodbye you toothless old bastard" David said as he flew up to freedom and away from this hell. He could almost taste the food, the bad coffee and even the acid rain of New London.

PART 3:

New Job Prospects

13

It was a few days later that David heard back from his new boss. He took an early morning walk through the bustling streets of New London. The neon lights burning into his skull once more. The people nearly knocking him over as they passed him, going about their own, personal, important affairs.

"Oh, how I missed this" he found himself saying out loud.

He was home.

His hand started to vibrate. His Samsung 5000, a phone he had built into his hand the day before, it's holographic lights glowing, his new boss was contacting him. He bent his thumb inwards to take the call.

A holographic image of his boss popped up.

"Is this David?"

"Yeah."

"The David that came so highly recommended

CHAPTER 13

by Paddy in the colony?"

"Yeah."

"Good, do what you need to do then meet the contact in New Soho, I'll call you later with a precise location."

Before David could say ok, the boss hung up and the image disappeared.

"Ok," he said under his breath "gotta see Dr Davies anyway."

It was about 10am when he got to the back alley surgery. The neon sign on the door said they were taking walk in appointments so David walked to the counter and put his name down for an optic fitbit upgrade.

Around an hour later he was sat in the operating chair.

"Ah, Mr Wright, back for an upgrade I see."

"What am I paying for here?" David asked.

"Well," Dr Davies began as he pulled up his swivel chair, "this, Mr Wright, is cutting edge technology. All the benefits of an ocular fitbit but without the clunky hardware. All for only £599."

The old bastard drives a hard bargain, David thought.

"What does it do, exactly?"

"Well, Mr Wright, it connects to your brain via

your optic nerve so any app you want to use just think it and it pops up in your heads up display, none of this speaking out loud anymore," his breath stank of cigarettes and bad coffee, "and as a special offer I can hook it up to your Samsung 5000 and it can even tell you how many bullets you have, for an extra fee of course."

"How much extra are we talking here?"

"£199."

"Ok, put me under and hook me up Dr."

Dreamy vibes. His skin vibrating to the kaleidoscope images dancing before him. Then he was five again. His mother reading him Alpaca Saves Christmas on Christmas Eve. Kaleidoscope images and skin vibrating again. He was eleven. First day of high school. Thoughts of promise, a new future lay before him. One that he couldn't possibly imagine.

"David?" a voice said. His mother's voice maybe?

"David?" it said again, this time more masculine.

"David?!"

He awoke. His left eye socket stinging slightly.

Pain shot through his arm, down his wrist and into his hand.

CHAPTER 13

"The pain should subside in about eight or nine days," Dr Davies said "take painkillers and it should ease a little."

David got up from the operating chair, paid the bill and left.

It was raining again when he got outside. His hand vibrated again and his boss's image popped up on his optic fitbit. It's working already? He thought.

"David," he said, "meet the contact outside the Neon Potato in New Soho in about an hour, his name is Alejandro."

"I know him," David said, "met him before I went down."

"Good," said the boss, sarcastically "then you'll have so much to catch up on."

The boss hung up and David made his way to the Neon Potato. He figured he'd get a drink while he waited.

The Neon Potato was a hive of activity. People dancing and grinding to the synthetic beats that blasted through the speakers. David was at the bar nursing his favourite whiskey with coke, no ice, no lemon. He saw Alejandro strut into the club wearing a pink suede suit with the sleeves rolled up, a white vest, white slip on shoes, a gold chain round his neck and rings on his fingers. David had a flashback to the greasy bastard popping him in the nose, he wasn't as well dressed back then. He must've gone up in the world. He still had the biomechanical arm though , David could tell as it now had a nice gold finish to it.

On his arm was the punk hooker, only now she had red hair not purple, she still wore those fishnets though. Her green UV lipstick shimmering in the blue light. She licked her lips as she scoped the bar for potential customers. Alejandro made a beeline for David at the bar.

He clocked the barman.

"A beer and whatever he's having," he ordered before turning to David "so you're the new guy huh?"

David turned to look at him.

"Holy shit!" Alejandro laughed, "I know you, I fucking do! I popped you a few weeks back haha! What's happening? Where you been?"

"The surface," David replied "I killed a cop."

"Damn bro," said Alejandro "you cold! The boss said you like ice" he slapped David on the back with his gold plated biomechanical arm and laughed.

"You wouldn't be so tough pre-augmentation"

CHAPTER 13

David thought.

"Anyway holmes, I'm here to show you" said Alejandro.

"Show me what?"

"The tricks of the trade my man! I need someone to take over while I hit the big leagues! I got a seat at the table!"

"What table?"

Alejandro laughed.

"You ain't been in the game long have you," he said "the big table....where the big guys at"

"I see," David said "the big table."

He finished his drink just as Alejandro got his and walked towards the back.

"Hey man where you goin'?" shouted Alejandro.

"Little boy's room!" David shouted back.

"Well hurry up, we got work to do!" he shouted back and took a swig of his beer.

Outside it was still raining and David was in a foul mood. He could tell he was going to hate this assignment. But he had bills to pay and this was the only legal way he knew how.

He did a background check on Alejandro on his optic fitbit.

Alejandro Hernandez Victor Hector Jones. "Jesus," David thought, "I better stick to Alejandro for now. Let's see, jailed for armed robbery when he was twelve, committed his first murder when he was fifteen, been stopped for traffic violations and suspected pimping in certain areas of New London. The New Krays know how to pick 'em."

Suddenly he heard the barman shout.

"Hey! You can't take that out with you!"

David turned to see Alejandro at the door with his beer.

"What the fuck you gonna do?" Alejandro shouted back, trying to be intimidating, but that shit only worked on his women because, as he was shouting at the barman, a big, black hand placed itself on his chest and the doorman, Big Pete, said "you're not allowed drinks outside sir."

"Hand off the chain chocolate boy!" Alejandro shouted "it cost more than you make in a month, I'm with the New Krays up in here!" the doorman pulled his hand away quickly.

"That's what I thought" said Alejandro, glorified in victory.

New London was a hotbed of different colours, creeds and nationalities. Even though Alejandro was Portugese, he faked an American accent because he thought it made him sound tough. He was from the Portugese slums south of New

CHAPTER 13

Battersea, but he made his living in New Soho because anyone could. With the right connections and the right amount of money, you could become a king in New Soho. You just need to find a product, a demographic and exploit it. That's what Alejandro did. That's why he's going to the big table. He earned it and David respected that. What he didn't respect was his treatment of women. Especially the ones in his employment.

"Shit beer anyhow," Alejandro said, spitting it out "time for Davey-boy to watch and learn."

The punk hooker followed them out and Alejandro said to her "you find a John?"

"No," she said, sheepishly.

He raised his hand and she flinched.

"Get the fuck back to work then Tiffany!" he shouted.

David remained silent, he couldn't blow his cover no matter how much he wanted to beat the shit out of Alejandro.

"You see?" Alejandro said, grinning, his teeth covered in gold "that's how you treat people who be tryina' fuck with yo money. Never let 'em leave without a John."

David nodded, all the while wanting to wipe that grin off his face with a right hook. Who knew what he did to those women behind closed doors.

"What do we do now?" David asked.

"We wait."

"For what?"

"For her to leave with a John, then we collect the money when they done."

"I see."

About half an hour later, Tiffany left with a fat, balding businessman who looked about fifty. They went down an alley and David and Alejandro followed them.

14

Ten minutes later, Alejandro was counting his money with a gold plated smile.

"When do I meet the boss?" David asked.

"You don't," Alejandro replied, "the boss meets you. Now shut the fuck up I'm countin'."

When he finished, Alejandro handed a pittance to Tiffany and kept the rest for himself.

No wonder he can afford his clothes, jewelry and fancy dental work.

When all was said and done for the day, David returned home to find he had a message on his answer phone. It was 2056 and David still had an answer phone. Why didn't they just call his mobile? It was Diane. She wanted to see David at the office immediately, he sighed and put his rubber trench coat back on, grabbed his house keys and got a taxi pod over to the police station. He had to be careful he wasn't followed or his cover would be blown.

Taxis were surprisingly discrete when it came to

their customers. They had cloaking technology and could even administer first aid if the customer was on their way to the hospital.

David got to the office about five minutes later as the taxi pod took a quick route. Diane was waiting in the coffee room.

"To what do I owe the pleasure?" he asked her.

"I want to know what you've learned so I can relay it to Captain Lee when he gets back from his holiday in the outer orbit."

In 2056, space travel was a popular form of holidaying as the novelty for the super rich had worn off by 2043. It reminded David of the European package holidays that arose in the mid-twentieth century.

"Well I learned how to pimp, that's about it apart from the fact that Alejandro is getting a seat at the big table."

"What big table?"

"The one with the big guys, apparently, I'm still working on it, I should have more for you soon, just gotta try and get a meeting with the boss, I've only spoken with him on the phone so far."

"Have you pressed Alejandro for a meeting?"

"Just enough to express an innocent interest, not enough to blow my cover."

CHAPTER 14

"Good, keep at it and let me know if you find anything else out about this big table."

"Will do."

David left and got another taxi pod back to his apartment wondering why this conversation couldn't have taken place over the phone. But he guessed his phone could be bugged.

He yawned when he got back home. It'd been a long day and he was tired so he had a shower and got into bed to sleep. Suddenly he was woken up by his hand vibrating. He answered it and it was the boss.

"I wanna meet, someone should be at your apartment in twenty minutes, be ready" he said and hung up. David wiped his face to try and wake up and got back dressed again. He was tired but he had to jump at this opportunity to meet the man behind the phone calls.

He called Diane and her image in his fitbit resembled someone who was very tired also but had to stay in the office for an extra hour.

"Diane, I got a meeting with the boss."

"That was quick, do you think Alejandro put in a good word for you at this table?"

"Maybe, he owes me for popping me in the nose."

"What?" Diane said, barely awake.

"Nevermind," David said and hung up.

Fifteen minutes later, his doorbell rang. He pressed the peephole button in his door frame and a holographic image of some big, brawny guy stood there, flickering. He pressed the intercom.

"Who is it?" asked David.

"Hugo," the caller answered, "I'm here to take you to the boss."

15

David was amazed, as they pulled up to the house of his new boss, at the sleekness of everything. He could definitely tell that the owner of this house was rich, wealthy even. The columns of the front porch reached a good twenty five feet and resembled the White House from what David saw in the history books found in one of the few libraries still open in New London. It was raining still and the lights from inside shimmered a golden white on his face as he got out of the car and approached the house. He was greeted at the door by a seemingly inebriated, skinny woman wearing a silver sequin dress, silver earrings in the shape of an isosceles triangle dangling from each ear, a gold necklace with a locket dangling down her tanned cleavage, her bleach blonde hair permed to resemble Marilyn Monroe and her face, creased with age and the same dark colour as her cleavage. She held a martini glass and sipped.

"Are you here to see Harold?" she said, her accent put her in the wealthy part of New London. Born with a silver spoon.

"Yes madam I am" David replied.

"He's in his office," she turns and points behind her, "Hugo will take you."

"Thank you," David said as he entered the house following Hugo.

The office was just as opulent and grandiose as the rest of the house. Harold was sitting in a large, clam shaped, navy blue velvet chair behind a large, mahogany and red table with edges made of white gold. He was old, David thought, with receding gray hair tied in a ponytail at the back with a red silk ribbon. His gray fu manchu beard twitched slightly as David came in, and he smiled. His suit was made of dark, black and red velvet with red lining on the lapels.

"Nice to meet you sir-" David began but Harold raised his hand to stop him.

"Harold, please," he said and lowered his hand, resting it on the table.

His accent, like the woman who greeted David, put him in the wealthy part of New London but it felt forced so David thought he was from elsewhere. Her bit of rough maybe? David quickly and

CHAPTER 15

discreetly did a background check on Harold on his fitbit.

Harold Butters, did time for conspiracy to commit organised crime and murder, served a week before his money bought him a ticket off the colony and back into society. Nothing known about his upbringing or where he grew up except that he was an orphaned at the age of six.

Hugo quietly made his way to the window of the room and stood watch over the meeting.

"Does Hugo make you nervous?" Harold asked.

"Not at all," David replied.

"Good, now we can get to business, I've brought you here because you come highly recommended by not only Paddy but Alejandro too, How is the Padster these days?"

"You know, torn between two things, money and women."

"Ah yes," Harold sat back in his chair and his smile widened, exposing a full set of pearly whites. He obviously didn't fight his way to the top like you had to on the colony.

Harold made a pyramid with his fingers, showing a signet ring on his wrinkly pinky. His smile was gone now, replaced by an ice cold, stern face. His hand then broke away, signalling for David to sit on a plush, gold coloured chair in front of the desk. David sat with a thump as he soon realised that the chair, although nice and comfortable, was built to be lower than the table. Some sort of power complex David thought.

"Now," Harold began, "I know you're under Alejandro at this time, but he's going up in the world now and I need a replacement, no, I WANT a replacement." his boney finger pointed at David. "That's where you come in, I need you to take up the mantle," his boney finger clenched into a fist and he raised it as if he was picking something really heavy up, "and take the reins."

"I can do that," David said.

"Good," Harold said "you start Monday."

David woke up the next morning and opened his curtains. Raining. He got dressed and had breakfast then put his rubber trench coat on and headed out. He caught an electric bus pod down to the Portuguese slums to meet Alejandro and they were just that. Slums. Shanty towns of corrugated iron roofs held up by beams of wood, barely standing next to weather worn tents. No wonder Alejandro wanted to get the hell out of this place. And do anything to achieve that it seemed. He spent about an hour looking for him, weaving his

CHAPTER 15

way past beggars, thieves, hookers and pimps, until at last he came upon a caravan. Alejandro was sitting outside drinking a beer underneath a corrugated iron roof. Tiffany came out as soon as David arrived and flashed him a smile. Her left eye was black and she missed a tooth.

"Any more than that'll cost ya," Alejandro joked, "ain't made of money."

Bastard, David thought behind a reciprocated smile as Alejandro finished his beer and threw the bottle away.

"Get the fuck back in and put some make up on to hide that black eye bitch," Alejandro shouted "we got work to do."

And he stood up, straightened his suit and reached his golden hand out to meet David's.

David reluctantly took it and they shook once.

They were in New Soho again and David, Alejandro and Tiffany, heavily made up, were walking the rainy streets looking for Johns. It wasn't long until they found one. A hipster with a bald head and handlebar moustache. Tiffany took him down an alley and David turned to Alejandro expecting them to follow.

"Go fetch," said Alejandro "I'll watch."

When David got to the end of the alleyway, he

couldn't see any sign of Tiffany and her hipster John. Suddenly, from behind a dumpster, the hipster screamed and retreated backwards, his skinny jeans round his ankles.

Tiffany followed, pulling up her fishnets and hot pants.

"You ever try that again," she screamed "and Alejandro will kill you motherfucker! Understand?"

"What's happened?" David asked.

"He's got a knife," she said "wanted to press it against my neck as we screw."

Suddenly, the hipster pulled his jeans up and drew his blade. David made ready as he lunged at him, swiping. David maneuvered out of the way and brought his foot up to meet the hipster's stomach, winding him and causing him to double over and drop the knife. Alejandro came in from the street, attracted by the commotion and grabbed the hipster by the scruff with his gold plated biomechanical arm. Smiling, he used his free, natural arm to punch the hipster in the face. Blood and teeth flew through the air and the hipster was down. Alejandro dug through the hipster's pockets while he was unconscious. Nothing but a credit and fifty sub credits.

"Damn prick," Alejandro said "not even enough

CHAPTER 15

to pay for Tiffany's time."

"We should hide the body," said David.

"He's just blacked out," said Alejandro "he'll wake up soon, cashless, toothless and more the wiser."

Alejandro pocketed the money and all three left the alley.

"We need a drink," said Alejandro "I'm buyin'."

16

In the Neon Potato, the two guys ordered their drinks as Tiffany got to work on the clientele.

David felt the adrenaline from the altercation still coursing through his veins and his leg was shaking. Alejandro noticed this and laughed.

"Haven't fought much eh esse?" he said, between chuckles "in the slums, all we do is fight. Hard life, straight up."

They got their drinks and sat at a table.

"So where are you from holmes?" asked Alejandro as he took a sip of beer, "here I am talkin' bout my life, what 'bout chu?"

"I'm from the east end, before the war, but now I have a place in Aurora Heights."

"Woah, look at chu!" Alejandro said, impressed "Aurora Heights, what chu do before the pen? Police Officer?

David nearly choked on his drink. Shit he thought.

CHAPTER 16

"No , I was a businessman," he lied "worked for the Sugar Corporation, found a female pig in bed with my wife, killed her, got sent down, released on good behaviour and now I'm here."

"Shit," said Alejandro "that's some story" he took another sip of his beer.

Soon after, on their third drink, Tiffany left with a John and David followed while Alejandro finished his beer. In the alleyway, again behind a dumpster for real privacy, she went down on the John for about half an hour and he paid handsomely for it. Sixty credits. David took thirty and gave thirty to Tiffany. She looked up at him, shocked.

"Don't tell Alejandro," he said and winked.

Back in the slums, Alejandro invited David in to "kick it" and David obliged. All that night they drank, talked and smoked "Angel Dust".

David sat back in his chair and admired his surroundings. The caravan was kept surprisingly tidy, for a slum anyhow. Tiffany's handiwork David thought before the effects of the alcohol and the Angel Dust began to kick in and the caravan pooled away and spiralled into nothingness. He saw the kaleidoscope images again, dancing, moving, and his skin vibrating even more so than when he was under anesthetic at Dr Davies' office.

"God ," David said to the kaleidoscope, rubbing his face, "I'm so goddamn high."

Alejandro laughed and it echoed all over David's whole world and morphed into dial up internet sounds.

Then nothingness again.

Then he was back in the caravan. He was by himself and everything had a green tint to it. The complete silence ringed in his ears. His mother appeared from nowhere, shaking her head, looking disappointed.

"You were such a good police officer," she said "now look at you."

"I am a good police officer." he said on the verge of tears.

He heard a faint voice shouting "WHAT?!!"

He realised what he just said and the voice became louder.

"WHAT THE FUCK?!!" it said.

He came to, confused and disorientated.

He looked up and Alejandro had a gun to his face.

"I fucking knew it," Alejandro growled through clenched teeth.

"I...it's not what you think," David tried to

CHAPTER 16

explain "I was a pig but then I went into business."

"Likely story esse," Alejandro said "should go nicely on your headstone."

"What's going on?" said a voice behind them.

It was Tiffany, she'd just been dying her hair blue, it suited her David thought.

"This pen dijo is a pig," Alejandro said, "get on the phone to Harold, tell him we got a rat."

He turned to Tiffany who was looking shocked.

David seized the opportunity and grabbed Alejandro's arm, wrestling the gun out of his grip and aimed it.

Tiffany came back with the phone. She was just about to ask for Harold when David aimed, his optic fitbit training a red marker on her head, and fired, killing her instantly. Alejandro lunged for him and David blew him away too.

Cleaning his prints off the gun, he placed it into Alejandro's lifeless hand and left without saying a word.

17

When he got back home, David sighed. What had he just done? Killed the only man who could get him closer to Harold Butters than he already was. He had to take his mind off it and come back to thinking about what he was going to do with a clear head. A shower, he thought, gotta take a shower. He stood in the shower for an hour. Letting the hot water run down his back. "What am i gonna do?" he found himself saying out loud.

When he got out and was dried, his hand vibrated and Harold's image popped up in his optic fitbit.

"David!" he said "Alejandro's been killed, did you hear? Where were you?!"

"I haven't seen him all day," David lied.

"Weren't you supposed to be shadowing him while he taught you the biz?"

"No not today," David said "he said he had other people to see."

CHAPTER 17

"That's strange, somebody swore they saw you three together, one of the Johns."

David gulped. Shit, he thought, Harold can't see me can he?

"Must've been mistaken," he said "I've been home all day."

"Hmmm," Harold looked through squinted eyes at David, as if he was trying to make up his mind if David was lying or not, "must be just mistaken identity I guess."

"Yeah," laughed David "I get that a lot."

He decided a walk would be his best bet to help him decide where to go from here. Harold's call had eased his mind a little. At least he's not been pushed out of the circle yet. The streets were quieter than usual. Hardly a soul to see. He checked his HUD in his optic fitbit. 10pm. He decided to go to New Soho and try to relax. He got on the bus pod, paid and sat down.

"David," a voice behind him said.

It was Diane. David was never so pleased to see her.

"What are you doing here?" he asked.

"I heard about Alejandro, was that you?"

"I had to," he said "he was about to blow my cover, actually it was more Tiffany was about to blow my cover, had to take care of her then he lunged at me and I had to take care of him."

"Damn," she said, a slight smile on her face "you are cold."

When he got to New Soho and said goodbye to Diane, David wandered the streets. He didn't want to go to the Neon Potato as they knew him now so he decided to try other establishments. There were enough of them to pick from. The Drunk Flamingo, the Flying Dutchman (nautical themed, of course), the Purple Bird. He decided to go there as it was dark and he liked the name. The Purple Bird lived up to expectations as the entire place was lit with purple neon and UV lights. He sat at the bar and ordered a drink.

He sat with his back to the bar and inspected the patrons with his optic fitbit. Not a criminal in the joint which was unusual for New Soho, normally there were a few rapists and muggers and maybe a pimp or two. Working the same place could be dangerous if you were in the pimping trade, you tried your best not to step on anyone's turf. He turned back to the bar when his drink came, whiskey and coke. An ambient song came on the speakers, not as loud as it was in the Neon Potato. It was a social place rather than a club. You could actually hear the person next to you here.

David drank his drink in one gulp and it hit him rather quickly. His hand vibrated again. It was Hugo.

"The boss wants to see you," he said "it's urgent."

Then he hung up.

"Social bunch" David said, and left the Purple Bird behind, he didn't think he was going to return.

When he got to Harold's house, he sat in the plush chair and waited for the boss to return from doing whatever it was that he was doing. I wonder what he wants, David thought.

"Sorry to keep you waiting," a voice behind him said. It was Harold.

"The wife likes tennis," he said "beats me every time."

"I'm sure you'll win sometime," said David.

"I'm sure I will," Harold said, sitting down behind his desk, "now, down to business, I'm sure you're wondering what was so urgent."

"I am actually," David said.

"I've decided to promote you," Harold said "from pimp to enforcer."

"Who's gonna take my place?"

"You don't need to worry about that, it's being

handled."

"By who?"

"I told you, you don't need to worry about that, you will go with Hugo, he'll show you the ropes."

Hugo smiled.

"Ok," David said.

"Right," said Hugo as they walked down the bustling, rainy street "we're gonna start you off with a light debt collection job. The person we're gonna see owes Harold three thousand credits, his business was going under and needed the money, but now he's booming he can afford to pay back."

"Who is it?" David asked.

"Foo Yong Lee, he owns a sushi bar here in New Soho," said Hugo.

When they got there, Foo Yong was closing up for the night.

"Ah Mr Hugo," he said, "I didn't know you were coming, I closing now, no sushi sorry."

"We're not here for sushi," Hugo said, "we're here because you owe Harold, time to pay up or we break something."

Foo Yong said something in Japanese and wiped his forehead with a cloth.

"Ok," he said, "I get money now."

He went in the back and brought out a suitcase.

CHAPTER 17

"Well," David said, "that's the easiest three thousand credits I ever made."

"Ninety five percent goes to Harold," Hugo said, "we get two point five each."

"I see," David said.

When David got home, he had a shower. His hair was starting to grow back thankfully. He looked at his prison number tattoo and remembered Tori, Bruno, The Boss, Paddy, Ricky and Georgey-Boy. The thought of Bruno made him shudder. He wondered if anyone found the bodies of Bruno and Tori, if The Boss had her little black book again, if the New Krays survived the battle.

When he got out of the shower, he turned the TV on. There was a news report on the 'tragic' deaths of two individuals found in the Portuguese slums. A muder/suicide they said, but David knew that the police would find the truth soon. He knew the process all too well. He walked to his window, through the rain he saw the various denizens of New London going about their various affairs. The neon lights of New Soho in the distance, dancing in the raindrops slowly sliding down his window. It was night time now and he knew the creeps would come out to play. He got dressed and left for New Soho. he had a job to do.

His hand vibrated, the image of Harold popped up in his HUD.

"I need you to collect four hundred credits from a taylor in the New West End, Albert Honeysworth, he's got a place on the corner, big white neon sign, can't miss it."

"Ok Harold."

When he arrived, Albert Honeysworth was closing up for the night.

"Honeysworth," David called out "you owe Harold."

"How much?" Honeysworth stammered.

"Four hundred credits," David said "pay up."

Honeysworth dug deep in his pockets and produced a fifty credit note, scrunched up.

"That's not enough," David said, looking down at the note with an air of disappointment.

"Ok," Honeysworth said, he was shaking now.

"I've got more in the register inside," he said, unlocking the padlock with a chip in his wrist. It glowed blue and there was a click to signify that it was unlocked.

When they entered, David noticed that the suits inside looked pretty expensive, so expensive in fact that Honeysworth probably didn't even need the money that he borrowed.

CHAPTER 17

Gambling addiction maybe?

Honeysworth opened the register with the same chip in his wrist that he used to unlock the shutters out front. He gave David three hundred and fifty credits and David pocketed it and left.

It was already daylight by the time David got to Harold's. God he was tired. Harold was sitting down to breakfast, bacon and eggs, when Hugo showed David into the kitchen.

It was quite a bright, airy room they were standing in. White walls, white floors, white counters. It almost looked sterile. Harold was wearing blue silk pyjamas under a scarlet robe.

"I had a call," he said, "Honeysworth was very shaken by your encounter with him, said you were quite rude."

"I only did as Hugo showed me," David said.

"Oh it wasn't a criticism," Harold said, "I was about to say good work, now do you have my money?"

David handed it over and kept the fifty for himself, which Harold didn't mind, he knew David needed his cut.

"A petty amount I know," Harold said as he was counting the money, "but if you don't keep on track with these people they begin to take advantage and you have to start making examples."

"Familiarity breeds contempt," David said and Harold smiled.

"Exactly," Harold said.

18

David was half asleep when he arrived home. He made himself a sandwich and watched TV before going to bed. In his dream he was in a field, he was six, his mother's hand was in his. He looked up at her smiling face. She had something in her other hand. A kaleidoscope.

"Here, David," she said "look through this."

He did so and saw all manner of colours as he slowly turned the tube. Blue, red, green, purple, silver.

Suddenly he heard a scream, he looked away from the lovely colours. His mother was on the ground, a smoking hole in her forehead. Then he wasn't in the field, he was in his mother's apartment. He was fifteen, and his mother was dead. At this he woke up screaming in a cold sweat. He rubbed the sleep and sweat from his face and noticed, in the blue light of the moon, that it was still raining.

"Shit," he said under his breath and he got up and had a shower.

It was soon enough that he got to Harold's mansion. He'd walked this time, so he took in the exterior scenery. He entered through a guarded gate and walked on a gravel driveway through a lush garden, rich with every kind of flora you could still get after the war. It was still raining so David didn't take in too much of his surroundings. What he did see though was a replica statue of David. He laughed at the situation.

He was met at the door by the woman who he assumed was Mrs Butters, but he couldn't be sure.

"Here to see Harold, I take it," she slurred, again drinking out of the martini glass. She wore a gold version of what she wore last time he saw her.

"Yes mam," David said, "is he in his office?"

"He's in his study, yes" she said.

David thanked her and entered the house.

"Mr Wright, as I live and breath," Harold said as David entered the office, "here for another job already?"

"Gotta keep active," David replied.

"Ok," Harold said "there's a certain individual who owns a club here in the West End, owes me a substantial amount, fifty thousand credits, you'll

CHAPTER 18

get your cut as per, that's if you make it past his door staff and his armed guards."

"What's the club called?" asked David.

"The Golden Pineapple," Harold replied "it has a sign shaped as a-"

"Golden pineapple?" David interrupted.

"That's it," Harold continued, "go there now, they should just be opening."

He got to The Golden Pineapple as he left a taxi pod, it was busy outside so David assumed this was a fancy place. He got up to the door and was stopped by the doorman. He flashed him a fifty and was allowed in.

"That was simple enough," he found himself saying out loud.

The club was nearly at full capacity, he did background checks on everybody. Nearly all of them were Neo Yuppies, out to have a good time probably, this was their turf. The UV lights were shining blue and the lasers flashed green, then red, the green again. The music was nearly deafening. The office was towards the back and was guarded by two big guys with AK47s. He felt for the pistol that Harold had given him before he left. Still there. He breathed a sigh of relief and carried on.

He got to the office door and one of the armed

guards stopped him.

"Where are you going'?" he said.

"To meet Mr Danny Parks," David said "he owes Harold."

"He owes shit," the armed guard said and aimed at David.

David took a step back and put his hand under his coat to get his gun but stopped when he remembered where he was and what was being aimed at him. He couldn't open fire here, and he'd be blown away before he could get a shot in.

"Look," David said, "I just need to see him for a second ok? If Harold says he owes then he owes."

"I don't care," the armed guard said "you ain't getting past me."

David thought it was a lost cause, that he'd have to return to Harold empty handed, fuck that he thought and went outside.

Outside, he noticed there was a side alley so he snuck behind the club and found a sliding window to the bathroom. It was open. He climbed through and just as he was landing two Neo Yuppies entered. They stared at David, and David stared back. David produced his pistol and the two Neo Yuppies left the room, shocked.

Before leaving the bathroom, he pocketed his

CHAPTER 18

pistol. When he left he noticed that the bathroom led to the kitchen and then to a balcony outside, so he walked that way, hoping against hope that he could find a side way to get into Danny Parks' office.

He got to the balcony with no trouble at all. He looked round each corner. There was an opening to the left that went back inside, hopefully to the office. He looked down off the balcony and saw a sewage river flowing off the side of New London. He climbed over the railing and entered the window. He found himself in a hallway decorated by faux graffiti and lit by a single, flickering bulb. Walking along it he realised that he'd bypassed the armed guards outside by the fact that the door they were guarding was to his left and closed. He could hear the music clearly through the door. He looked to his right and there was a doorway, held open by a drinks crate and through a hallway where, he assumed, Danny Parks' office was. He made his way quietly down the hallway and found himself greeted by another door guarded by armed men. They didn't ask questions though, and opened fire right there and then. David ran for cover in the opposite direction and hid behind a corner, firing back. Behind him he heard the door opening and gunfire and screams coming from the club. He turned round and opened fire at the armed guards, killing one and fatally wounding the other. He turned back round and resumed fire. They exchanged fire until David was sure they were dead. Again he made his way down the hallway to the door. A sign said Mr Parks' office, no unauthorised entry in red. He felt a stabbing pain in his left shoulder, felt it and drew his hand away. It was covered in blood, he must've caught one in his shoulder coming in. Ignoring the pain, he kicked the door down and aimed. He found Danny Parks curled up and crying, actually crying, in the corner.

"You owe Harold, Danny," David said, lowering his gun "and it's a lot so pay up, bitch."

"Ok, ok, the money's in the safe, over there," he pointed to the safe in the corner "the code is three, four, four, three. Please don't kill me!"

David opened the safe, three hundred million, David looked about the room for a bag big enough to carry the loot until he stopped and found a black sports bag big enough to carry that amount. He packed the bag full and zipped it up all the while Danny Parks moved to his glass desk in the middle of the room. He went through the drawers and found his machine pistol and fired at David who, in turn,

CHAPTER 18

fired back, hitting Danny Parks between the eyes.

Blood hit and ran down an expensive looking oil painting that hung behind the office desk.

An alarm blared over the speaker phones. David wanted to know what this was. Reinforcements? Another acid rainstorm? One was due. He called Harold who said "get out of there, find a shelter and a pod should be with you in ten minutes. And David? Bring me my money."

He left The Golden Pineapple which was now deserted following the gunfire. A weather report appeared in his fitbit. Acid rainstorm imminent, customer suggestion: find shelter it said, then a map of New London popped up and all the locations of the purpose built shelters were highlighted by electric blue speech bubbles saying the address of each of them. He picked the nearest one which was on the corner. Ten minutes later, the acid rain was easing into normal rain and as promised, the pod turned up and David got in.

A friendly, robotic voice spoke to him.

"It seems you, or someone in your party is injured," it said "do you wish to go to one of the many hospitals for treatment?"

"No," David replied "I wanna go to a residence owned by a Mr Harold Butters, please, I'll receive treatment there."

"Okey doke," the voice said, trying to sound human, "our estimated time of arrival will be exactly ten minutes."

When he arrived at Harold's office, he threw the bag on the table and sat down as Harold's personal nurse removed the bullet and stitched him up.

"I'm impressed, Mr Wright, barely a scratch on you, and look," Harold leaned over the table, opened the bag and looked up smiling, "you found my money."

"All present and accounted for? David asked, wincing in pain as the stitches were administered.

"Yes," Harold said, counting his money "apart from your bonus."

Hugo's smile, which had been beaming so far, stood there in the corner of the room, quickly left his face.

"Bonus?" David asked.

"Yes," Harold said "in consideration of your exceptional duties this evening. If I'm at all honest, I didn't expect to see you again, Mr Wright."

When he got home, David counted his earnings. Thirty thousand credits. Impressed at the payload, he put it in his wall safe, got undressed and went to sleep.

19

The next morning, David woke up to find it not raining. Shocked, he got dressed quickly and left his apartment. But, as sod's law would have it, it started raining as he left the Aurora Heights lobby, so he returned to his apartment to retrieve his rubber trench coat and umbrella.

The streets were busy as usual but David didn't mind as much now. He remembered the solitude of the colony and smiled, happy that he wasn't down there anymore. A weather report box popped up in his fitbit and it said acid rain was forecast for 4pm that day so David made a note of the nearest shelter and left for Harold's place to see if there were any more debts that needed collecting. He boarded the bus pod and left Aurora Heights for the day.

When he got to Harold's, there was indeed a job waiting for him. A Mr Ulysses Lee owed Harold a couple thousand credits hush money. Where did David know that name? It couldn't be Captain Lee.

A big place, New London, he guessed, names can be replicated. Jeez he even arrested two guys in a strip club one night, both called Aaron. He made his way to Mr Lee's houseblock in New Hampstead. It was a grand place too. The front door was painted black and had a gold knocker and letterbox, which was for more decorative purposes as nobody wrote letters anymore and there was a buzzer by the door.

He buzzed Lee's apartment.

"Hello," a tired voice greeted.

"I'm an associate of Mr Harold Butters," David said, "you owe him some money?"

"Not so loud, ok?" the voice said, "I'll come down and post the envelope under the door."

David waited, and after a while there was indeed an envelope with money inside posted under the door. Three thousand credits.

"That's all the money I have," a voice from behind the door said.

"Ok," David said "I'll bring this back to Harold and if any more is requested I'll be back for it."

He gave Harold the envelope. Harold counted and tutted.

"This isn't enough," he said, "not for the secret I'm keeping for him."

"What secret's that?" David asked, puzzled.

CHAPTER 19

"Well, David," Harold said, leaning back in his chair, "if I told you it'd cease to be a secret. But, for curiosity's sake, lets just say his….interests are a little unorthodox."

"Unorthodox legal?" David asked, "or unorthodox illegal?"

"The second one," he said.

"Ok," David said "how much more does he owe?"

"Another sixty thousand," Harold said.

David arrived back at Ulysses Lee's place.

Again he pressed the buzzer, and again the voice answered.

"Harold wants another sixty," David said "pay up or this fancy door won't be fancy for much longer."

"I'll come down," the voice said "and we can settle this face to face."

Minutes later the door opened.

"David?" the voice said.

It WAS Captain Lee.

"I think you'd better come in." he said, and David followed him inside.

They sat in a grandiose apartment. Walls filled with expensive works of art. A few Picassos and a few Dahlis amongst other treasures that David assumed Lee paid out his arse for. They were sat on stylish, white leather sofas and had tea from expensive china, resting on a glass, oval shaped coffee table.

The first words from Lee were "what's he told you?"

"Nothing really," David said, "just said your interests were illegally unorthodox."

Lee sighed.

"He's lying?" David asked.

"What do you think?" Lee replied, taking a sip from his tea.

"I think there's some truth to it," David said, "or you wouldn't be paying him."

"Now David," Lee said, "I don't want to be pulling rank in this situation, it's as dangerous to me as it is to you, I am a superior officer and-"

"Don't even bother, sir, what's this secret?"

"Her," Lee said, looking at his feet.

"Her what? Her who?"

"Look, she looked older than she was ok?"

David's eyes widened.

"You mean you-?"

"No, no," Lee pleaded, more to himself than to David, "I couldn't have….I can't….you can't"

Lee was getting visibly upset by this, on the

verge of tears.

"Oh...my...God," David said.

David got up to leave.

"David?" Lee said, "you won't tell anyone will you?"

"I won't," David said "but I can't say the same for Harold."

And with that, David left Captain Ulysess Lee, not knowing that he'll never see him alive again.

When David got to Harold's house, he mentioned what Lee had told him.

"An underage girl," Harold said, "he met her in the Outer Rings resort near Saturn, he did her while her parents were in the other room watching TV."

David was nearly sick. A man he looked up to in the force, a monster. This was no mistake of age. This was knowingly committing a crime.

"And now," Harold continued, "we have to let his secret out, for the sake of the countless other girls he's probably abused over his time as 'Captain of the police force'."

"And because he didn't pay you enough," David said.

"That too," Harold said, smiling pearly whites, like a predator who caught his prey. "I've been hiking up the prices for a while now, in the end I knew he'd run out of money, and time."

David got home that night clearly shaken and still a bit sickened by all of this.

He looked at some family photos, taken years ago it seemed, happy barbeques, Christmases, New Years Eve office party when David got up on his desk and sang the time warp on karaoke, and did the dance too. God those were fun times.

Who knew that one day, someone he trusted with his life, had beers with, seen on an almost daily basis, was a sex offender?

He put them away and got ready for bed.

As he was just drifting off, his hand vibrated. It was Diane.

"David, the Captain!!" she screamed "he's dead! Apparent suicide."

She started crying.

David didn't feel anything but relief and disgust.

Sure it was great that he's dead, but he won't come to justice and that bugged the hell out of him.

20

The next day, David was walking the streets of New Soho, looking for a new hangout spot. He happened upon a new place that just opened up. Jeffry's had an old looking aesthetic. It reminded David of the pubs in the old towns of his youth. With the brass glistening on the ends of the bar, which was a shiny oak colour. And the stools too. Real gastro pub experience.

He sat on a stool and felt the velvet greet his posterior, ordered a drink. They only had spirits and beer, so he ordered a whiskey. 'Real pub' he thought.

The barman, smiling, poured him a Jack Daniels and David sipped and enjoyed.

He was summoned once again to Harold's. He finished his drink and went catch the next bus pod. It was raining and cold but David didn't feel it. The whiskey had taken affect and David didn't just see the neon lights, but felt them too. It was like different levels of vibration, running all over his body. The bus pod arrived and David got on.

During the journey, David watched the raindrops fall down the window and remembered the old world. The one before the war. There was a pandemic then. Covid-19. You had to que up outside shops to get food. People were losing jobs. You had to wash your hands frequently to avoid infection. People wore masks and gloves to protect themselves and you had to remain two metres apart to prevent the spread of the virus. People were dying in the thousands and the government scientists were trying to find a cure. Then the war came. America was angry with China for not acting sooner to prevent coronavirus from their country, so they ceased all trading with China, so China reacted with a nuclear missile strike, nearly wiping America off the map. America fought back with their own missiles, nearly destroying the world in the process. A year or two later, the New London initiative was born and construction commenced with haste. People needed safety from the storms mother nature had exacted in response to the nuclear strikes by the world's two superpowers. In its infancy, New London wasn't any different from a bunker, same camping beds, grey, lifeless walls

CHAPTER 20

strewn with cables and pipes, but as more and more people came from different countries and cultures it bloomed into a floating metropolis.

And now it was exactly that. A metropolis. But it didn't come without it's bad eggs. As more and more immigrants came in, more and more gangs surfaced to take advantage of the easy life. One where you could make big credits in a small amount of time. That's where David and his team came in. They were set up to combat organised crime and that's what David had to remember. He was fighting it, not joining in.

He had to commit low-level crime in order to stop the high-level crime.

But crime is crime, in David's book, no matter how low-level it was, somebody always got hurt.

The bus pod stopped just outside Harold's place, and David heard the familiar air raid siren signalling an acid rain storm, so he hurried in and met Harold in his office. He didn't get to see much more of the house as he was small fish at the moment. 'But soon' he thought 'soon I'll be big fish and get to see more of this lovely house, and when the rain stops for a second I'll see the gardens too.'

When he got to the office, he sat on the plush chair again.

Harold was already there, he was on the phone to someone very important, it seemed. He still used a brass handheld telephone with a gold cradle and a turn dial. David sat and waited patiently for Harold to finish his conversation.

When he finally dropped the phone in its cradle, he looked at David suspiciously.

"That," he said at last, "was the chief of police, they want to see you, they say, from what they saw on the unfortunate Captain Lee's CCTV footage, you were the last one to see him alive. They want to speak with you."

"Ok," David said, a little shocked.

"Go now," Harold said, "Hugo will take you."

They made their way to the car when the acid rainstorm had passed and the normal rainstorm resumed.

"Boss wants you to lie," Hugo said, "lie through your back teeth, that you didn't know the ol' cap' was gonna off himself."

"I didn't," David said.

Hugo laughed.

"That's the way," he said.

They were at the police station quick enough. David went in, but in a way that he didn't show Hugo, he knew his way around. He walked up

CHAPTER 20

to the reception desk. There was a pretty woman working there tonight, about thirty and with blonde and blue hair tied up in a bun.

"DI Wright," she said, as she looked up and saw him, "you're supposed to be undercover right?"

"Act like you don't know me," he whispered, through clenched teeth.

She frowned, confused at his reaction, and mouthed 'what?'

"One of them," he jolted his head behind him, "is outside, in the car, act like you don't know me."

She made an expression that denoted understanding.

"How may I help you?" she asked, in her best polite but sounding slightly autonomous voice.

"I'm here," he said, normal volume now, "to see the chief, he said he wants to speak with me, damn pig."

"Ok, take a seat, he'll see you shortly."

David was sat in the waiting area for about an hour. It looked like a sterile doctor's office, with its white walls and its white ceiling, floors, tables, chairs, everything. White. White. White. After a further hour of waiting, David's eye began to hurt and his fitbit started to slightly malfunction.

" Note to self," he thought "see Dr Davies about

this."

"DI Wright?" a quiet voice behind him said.

He turned to see the chief's secretary. Another pretty woman with blonde and blue hair, this time it was in french braids.

"The chief will see you now," she said.

"Thank you," he said back.

As soon as he entered the chief's office, he was ordered to sit down. As he did, the chief leaned forward. He was a fat old bastard with acne scars on his cheeks and chin and he wore a bright blonde wig, (didn't anyone up top have any hair?).

"Now David," he said, a croissant still in his mouth, "I can call you David?," he swallowed

"I've been going over your progress with Diane on your assignment, she says you're making progress and I agree with her, would you agree also?"

"I've gotten in with them proper, but I'm just small fish at the moment, did a bit of pimping, that failed so I shot the guy teaching me the ropes because he was gonna blow my cover."

"The Portuguese slums murder/suicide."

"Now, Harold has me on debt collection and I don't know if that will go anywhere."

"And that's how you came upon Captain Lee?"

CHAPTER 20

"I was collecting-"

"Hush money, we know, we know all about Captain Ulysses Lee and his interests. Even if he thought we didn't know, we knew."

"Why wasn't he brought to justice in his lifetime?"

"Do you realise what that would do to the police community? Society at large?" the chief raised his arms as if he was holding out a rectangle shaped box.

"'Peedo copper in a high rise job and cushty apartment', press would have a field day with that. That's why we've gotta keep it on the downlow, and for your own protection we need to put you in the ol' drunk tank for the night, slap you about a bit so you get a nice shiner, then send you back to Harold nice and convincing that you've been defiant to our questioning methods."

"Ok," David said, "how much of a shiner?"

His cheekbone and eye socket started to swell. He wasn't enjoying this part of the deception. Whoomph! Another punch to his face and he spat some blood and a tooth to the ground. He was tied up in the drunk tank so he couldn't flinch. One of his team, Bennet, was the guy who was carrying out the fake interrogation. And he was enjoying it.

"That's enough," the chief said and Bennet sighed and stopped.

They untied him and told him to get some sleep and they'll get him up in the morning.

21

Soon enough, morning came and, true to their word, they woke him up and let him go.

Hugo was asleep in the car as David walked out.

David got in the car and slammed the door, waking Hugo up from a dream he was having about pretty cheerleaders, dancing their routines naked.

"How long was I out?" he said.

"I don't fucking know," David said, angryly, "I was in the drunk tank all night, getting my arse kicked for you and the boss."

"Woah! What's the matt-" Hugo thought better of finishing that question when he saw David's eye.

"Just take me home," he said, and Hugo drove him back to Aurora Heights.

When he got home, David sat on his sofa. He wasn't happy with his current predicament. Face all swollen, he showered. As he was drying, his hand vibrated. Harold wanted him to come over for lunch to discuss a new career path. Promoted again maybe? He got dressed and left.

Harold was shocked when he saw David's face.

"God," he said, "they must've beaten you something terrible."

"I told them nothing," David said.

"Good," Harold said, smiling.

Their food arrived and they ate in silence.

It was a delicate looking dish, David wasn't used to eating like this.

When they were finished, Harold put his napkin to his lips and spoke.

"So," he began, "what's on the horizon for David then?"

There was a long pause, as if David didn't think he'd actually have to answer the question. Or that if it was even directed at him, or just Harold thinking out loud.

Harold put his napkin on the table before continuing.

"I think," he said "you should be promoted, you've proven yourself to be a reliable, trustworthy person, I just need you to do another job for me," he looked at David through squinted eyes, "I need you to go to New Chinatown and pick up a package from someone."

CHAPTER 21

"Ok," David said "what kind of package?"

"Just a little something," Harold said.

The rain still fell in buckets as the bus pod pulled into Tanaka Street. The neon lights here made New Soho look drab in comparison. David disembarked and looked around. His fitbit flashed on his HUD and he saw out the corner of his eye the address that Harold had given him before he left. 368 Tanaka Street. He noticed it by the huge neon sign above the door. Tanaka Street's best noodle takeaway, it flashed.

"He wants noodles?" David asked himself.

He entered the building and went to the order desk.

"Order for Harold Butters," he said to the short, Asian lady behind the desk.

"You wait here," she said, in broken English, "I get order."

At this, she disappeared behind the kitchen and shortly reappeared with a parcel wrapped in plastic and held together by duct tape.

David took the parcel, thanked her then left to catch the next bus pod back to Harold's place.

While he waited, the rain was falling that hard he struggled to hear himself think. An Asian man was waiting there also. He looked young, no older than twenty four maybe? He fished a cigarette out of his pocket and offered David one. David took it and the young man offered to light it for him, David took the offer, not knowing what was about to happen. Suddenly three other young, Asian men appeared.

"Give us Harold's parcel!" one of them ordered, in perfect English.

"I can't do that," David said, "it's very important that I get this to Harold as soon as possible."

"Then you leave us with no choice," said the smoking Asian man.

Suddenly , they all produced a Stanley knife each and David ducked and dove to avoid the slashing movements. What was in this parcel that they needed so badly? Was this just a run of the mill mugging? Or was this something else entirely? David ran from the bus stop and into a clothes store and through to the back alley. He turned to see if they were following him. They were in the store, stabbing at clothes racks, hoping that he was hiding there. The store owner was shouting something in Chinese and they shouted insults back, then, disappointed in not finding him, they left. David released a breath he didn't know he was holding and returned to the bus stop. Thankfully it was empty and the bus pod was just arriving.

When he got to Harold's he threw the parcel on the desk. Harold looked up from a book he was reading and smiled.

"You got it then?" he asked.

"Yeah I got it," David said, a little pissed off, "mind telling me what's in this? I just nearly got mugged getting it for you, and they seemed to know it was for you because they mentioned you by name."

Harold put the book down, leaned forward, smiled, got a letter opener and slashed the parcel open. Pure China White spilled onto the desk.

"So that's what I've been carrying around with me," David said, "drugs, what if I got stopped?"

"Ah David," Harold said, "you worry too much and ask too many questions."

"I don't wanna get sent back to the surface," David said, "It's hell down there.

"Fair enough," Harold said, "now," he sat back in his chair and folded his arms, "about this promotion, how does advisor sound? You'll be at the same level as Hugo."

"Sounds good to me," David said.

Harold smiled.

When David got home, he video called the chief

and told him everything.

"If Harold is pushing pure China White then we're in deep shit," the chief said.

"I know," David said, "he's made me an advisor to him, so I'm getting close. It'll only be a matter of time before I have something really solid against him."

At that, the chief hung up and David went to sleep.

22

When he woke up, David felt refreshed and ready for the day ahead. He hadn't felt like this in a while. It was raining but he didn't feel down about it. As soon as he was washed and dressed, he went to his wardrobe. On top of it was a memory box. It was full of old photos and whatnot. He pulled out a kaleidoscope. His mother had given it to him before she died. He walked, with it in his hand, to his window and looked out. The rain was falling down the window and he thought it looked beautiful. He looked through the kaleidoscope. Many colours, all dancing before him. Seconds later, there was a knock at his door. He pressed the spyhole button with his thumb. It was Hugo.

"Time to go," Hugo said.

While they were driving, Hugo turned to David. "So," he said, "you were down on the colony?"

"Yeah," David said, "only a few weeks though."

"You meet my brother?"

"Could've done, what's his name?"

"Bruno."

David felt awkward. He hadn't the heart to tell him that his brother was dead. And that he'd killed him. Suddenly, David's hand vibrated again, it made him jump out of his skin. It was Harold.

"You and Hugo go to New Chinatown," he said "there's a person I want you to meet with. A new board member of the New Triads, I'll email you the address to your fitbit."

"Ok," David said.

Harold hung up.

"Where to?" Hugo asked.

"New Chinatown."

Hugo took a U turn and moments later they were on the bustling streets of New Chinatown.

They parked outside the address and entered. It was a hotel, in the fashion of old victorian England with gold and brass furnishings everywhere. The entrance danced neon gold and silver in the rain. They approached the desk and David looked on his HUD for the room number. Two forty seven. They asked what floor that number was on.

The man behind the desk was white and dressed like an old style usher. With his black and white tuxedo with a grey waistcoat and a black

CHAPTER 22

bowtie. His hair, grey and held down by what seemed a ton of hair gel. It glistened in the light.

"Room two forty seven," he said, as if he were royalty "is on the forty second floor sir."

They thanked him and took the elevator to the forty second floor.

Outside the room, they heard laughing inside, then a woman screaming. Maybe it was the police officer in him, but David felt the adrenaline surge through him, he was ready to kick the door down but he restrained himself as it would blow his cover. Hugo knocked on the door and the person inside shouted drunkenly something in Chinese. Moments later, the door opened to reveal a heavy-set Chinese guy, his hair black and tied up in a bun. His silk dressing gown barely covering his heavy frame and tied in the middle.

"Hello," he said, in a husky voice, "what you want?" his broken English not much of a barrier.

"Harold sent us," Hugo interrupted David, who was just about to speak.

"Harold?" the Chinese guy asked.

"Mr Harold Butters," David corrected Hugo.

"Ah," the Chinese guy said, the name suddenly dawning on him, "Butters-San."

"Yeah," Hugo said "and who are you?"

"I Chong Yu."

He invited them in. Inside the room was a four poster bed with white linen and purple silk duvets. On the bed was a naked, young-looking Asian girl, David felt uncomfortable, she couldn't be any more than thirteen.

They sat on a blue velvet sofa and Chong Yu poured them each a cup of sake.

"So what I do for Butters-San?" Chong Yu asked when he sat on the bed, he went to touch the young girl, but she shrank away from him. David noticed Hugo was smiling. That same smile Bruno had when he'd finished raping Tori. David felt a surge of unfathomable anger, but swallowed it.

"He's sitting on some product," Hugo said, "apparently some of your boys tried to take it from David here. He needs to know if we have parlay here in New Chinatown, and if we can maybe shift some of our own shit?"

"Maybe," Chong Yu said, "I think."

"Did you see how young that girl looked?" David said, when they left the hotel.

"Yeah," Hugo said "ripe."

"I wouldn't say that," David said.

"Well," Hugo said "what would you say?"

"Young," David replied "untouchably young."

CHAPTER 22

"Well , you know the Asians."

"I wouldn't say that either."

Hugo stopped and turned to David.

"What is it with you today?" he said.

David stopped, angry at himself when he realised what he'd said.

"Just not feeling that good," he said, "got up out the wrong side of the bed I guess."

Hugo looked like he understood and they carried on walking to the car, the wind and the rain battering them, the thunder rumbling like the drums of war.

23

The next day, David was again called into Harold's office. He went to sit down but Harold made a gesture that showed that's not what he wanted. So he stood.

"I want you and Hugo to go back to New Chinatown," he said, "I need you to talk with Chong Yu again about getting us that parlay to sell our product in New Chinatown."

"Ok," David said, and left the old man to his various affairs.

They got to New Chinatown in no time at all. The streets bustling with neon lights, people conducting commerce, street vendors hawking their wares. It was raining of course. It always rained it seemed. That didn't dampen the spirits of the street vendors though, they always seemed happy. As long as there were people to buy what they were selling, they were happy.

"Couldn't Harold talk with Chong Yu on the

CHAPTER 23

phone?" David asked, "it'd be easier than us risking our necks in this part of the city."

"We're here because he fucking desires it," Hugo said, alittle aggitated "so shut the fuck up."

"What's happening to us?"

"Whaddaya mean?"

"I mean yesterday me, today you, what's happening?"

"I may as well tell ya, I found out my brother's dead this morning."

"Dead?"

"Yep," Hugo looked at David, his eyes were beginning to well up but it looked like he was holding on by a thread so David didn't push it. He remained quiet for the rest of the drive to Chong Yu's place.

When they got there, David turned to Hugo.

"Just let me do the talking today," he said, "you're in no condition to haggle for a parlay."

Hugo nodded, silently.

David knocked on the door and moments later Chong Yu answered. He was in a suit this time. Black, white and grey, like the receptionist at the hotel the day before. He invited them in and they sat down in his living room.

"You want parlay in New Chinatown? You want

sell your drugs here?" he said.

They both nodded and Chong Yu started to laugh. Once he'd chuckled for a bit, Chong Yu became deadly serious.

"I give you parlay, you move freely in New Chinatown" he said, "but you no sell your drugs here, look somewhere else."

"Harold won't be pleased," David said, "he's got his heart set on this place."

"Triad no care what Butters-San think," Chong Yu said, "no drug sell here. We have own drug, we want money from own drug."

At that he pointed to his door.

"You leave now, I very busy," he said, and they left.

"FUCK!" Hugo screamed in the car as they drove back to Harold's place. Harold definitely won't be happy. David just kept his mouth shut the entire drive. He was upset that the deal didn't go to plan too as he didn't have anything on Harold anymore.

As they pulled into the drive, David noticed a posh new car parked by the door. A black Sedan 5000. He frowned as they passed it. 'Who owns that' he thought.

They walked into the office and Harold was

CHAPTER 23

standing by the window, looking out with his hands behind his back. He turned as they entered and smiled.

"David," he said lightheartedly, "you have a visitor, an old friend with some interesting news."

He looked toward the plush chair and David followed his gaze.

Sitting there, with a smile on her face, was the Supreme Boss from the colony.

David's heart leaped in his throat and he found himself mouthing 'what the fuck'.

"Hello David," she said, smiling "I was just telling Harold about our time together on the colony, and thanking him of course."

"Thanking him for what exactly?" David asked, incredibly nervous now.

"Why paying for her release of course," Harold interjected, "she was just telling me about how well you know each other, well enough to share secrets and life stories and the like."

"Ok," David stammered.

'Ok?' he thought, 'is that all you can say'?

"She was just telling me about the time you visited Hugo's brother Bruno. And about when you killed him, isn't that right Lisa?"

"That's right Harold," she laughed, "drowned

him in a bathtub, ugly way to go if you ask me."

David looked to Hugo, who was now staring at David, breathing deep and loud. The vein in his thick, muscular neck throbbing vigorously.

"I think," Harold said, "David should go home and think about what he's done, don't you think David? Or should I say DI David Wright?"

David backed away slowly before turning and running out the office. Hugo followed him part of the way, before Harold called him back.

When David got home, he struggled with the lock as his hands were shaking violently. He stopped, took a deep breath, then tried again. It unlocked easier this time and he entered his home, bolting the door behind him.

He video called the chief.

"Chief," he shouted "chief they know who I am, the operation's been compromised."

"Calm down," the Chief said "I'll send someone over to collect you. You'll be in protective custody."

"Ok," David said, hyperventilating.

CHAPTER 24

24

A few agonising hours later, there was a knock at David's door. Breathing a sigh of relief at the thought of being in protective custody, David answered and was met by a fist. He flew backwards and hit the floor with a hard thump. His head spinning, he tried to get up, only for Hugo to walk in and grab his lapels, throw him up against the wall and scream in his face.

"Harold said to go easy on you," he said "but, you killed my brother, you're a rat, and Harold ain't here."

"I'm sorry!" David whimpered.

Hugo then threw David across the room, his strength terrifying David who landed through his glass coffee table. Again, he tried to get up and fight back but, as he was rising, Hugo was on him, lifting him up with one arm and smashing him into the ceiling, then back down to the floor, then up to the ceiling again, before letting him drop to the floor with a hard bump.

"Aww shit," David slurred through a mouth full of blood.

He looked round for a weapon, and clocked his police issued beretta 9mm under the sofa. He began crawling agonisingly toward it.

"Where are you going?" Hugo laughed, and kicked him in the side, causing David to rise a few centimeters in the air. But David still kept at it, crawling slowly, Hugo kicked him again and again David rose a few centimetres in the air before landing with a bump.

Eventually, after a few more kicks, David got to his weapon, turned on his back, aimed and fired, catching Hugo in the neck. Hugo fell to the floor with a loud bump. Exhausted, David sat up, breathing heavily. Blood pouring down his face and shirt.

Suddenly, Hugo rose again and David aimed and shot him again in the chest. Hugo fell backwards and lay still.

He then heard a voice.

"FREEZE!" yelled this voice and David turned to see a uniformed police officer aiming his weapon at him.

"It's ok!" David slurred, tired out and a little

CHAPTER 24

dizzy following the altercation.

He got cleaned up. He was angry, angry as hell at Harold. David was gonna pay him a little visit. He loaded his gun, holstered it and walked out his apartment.

He didn't take a bus pod. He walked. All the way, through New Soho, through the Portuguese slums south of New Battersea, through the large, black, iron gates, right up to Harold's door and knocked slowly three times.

Mrs Butters answered. She saw the gun in David's hand and the look in his eye. She stepped aside and David walked in, slowly, and she ran to the phone to call for backup. He shot her in the back of the head and she fell to the floor in a clump. Two men ran into the lobby. And before they had a chance to even aim their weapons, he shot them too. He came to the hallway leading to Harold's office. There, he ran into three of Harold's bodyguards. They fired at him with AK47s and he hid behind one of the many columns that lined the hallway, firing back at the intervals while they loaded. Eventually, after a few minutes of firing back and forth, David heard the click of empty rifles. He checked his bullet count on his HUD. 'Eight bullets remaining'. He was going to have to aim right if he wanted enough to take out Harold. He heard footsteps running in the direction of the door at the other end of the corridor. He broke cover and fired, hitting two men in the back and the third in the neck. He stepped over them as they wriggled in pain on the floor.

When he got to Harold's office door, he stopped, an icon flashed on his HUD. 'Five bullets remaining' it said. He accessed an app on his fitbit's HUD which allowed him to have heat seeking vision. Suddenly everything became a dark shade of blue. He looked towards the door and saw Harold's multi-coloured form on the other side. It looked like he was holding something. David turned the heat seeking vision off, he wanted normal vision for this. He entered and Harold fired. David dove behind the plush chair for cover and Harold dove behind his desk.

"I thought you'd be dead, pig," Harold taunted, "obviously Hugo didn't have it in him."

"Oh he did," David called back, "I just killed the fucker."

"It's a shame, really, you had such promise, are you sure you're in the right profession?"

"If it means getting people like you off the street, I'm happy."

CHAPTER 24

"You know, Lisa told me about Tori, she sounded like a beautiful person."

"She was," David said, looking downwards.

"Why are we fighting like this?" Harold called, "lets just put our guns down and talk through this."

"Ok," David called "on three...one….two…... three!"

They both put their guns down and broke cover.

"See?" Harold said, smiling, "I can be trustworthy."

"Yeah," David said, "for an evil old codger you're pretty trusting yourself."

"Maybe too trusting," Harold said, "to a rat like you, a rat who's betrayed my trust."

At this, Harold unholsted a hidden gun he had up his sleeve and shot David, hitting him in the shoulder. David fell to the floor. Harold walked round his desk as David reached for his gun.

"You know," he said, "Tori may be looking down at us here. Looking down at you, wondering what she ever saw in you….I understand there was some chemistry between you both."

"I may not have loved her the way she wanted," David struggled to say, "but I still loved her."

David reached for his gun again and Harold

shot him in his leg. He screamed. Harold picked his gun and aimed.

"Well," he said, "you'll be together soon."

David successfully reached for his gun again, grabbed it, turned over on his back, aimed and fired, hitting Harold right between his eyes.

PART 4:

Epilogue

25

It was sunny when David left Harold's house. For the first time in a long while it was actually sunny, and he loved it. He walked out onto the street and looked around. There were heat waves dancing on the ground. Steam rising from the puddles. Not a cloud in sight.

"David?" he heard a familiar voice call. It was Diane.

"Diane," he said to her, "it's good to see you." He limped toward her.

"What happened?" she asked, shocked at the sight of him, bloody, bruised and tired.

"Got my arse kicked, got shot, twice, and I'm tired as fuck," he said, and smiled.

She smiled back, and suggested they went to the hospital.

It was a few days later when David returned home from work. He had a great time, Chong Yu went down to the prison colony for peadophilia and selling drugs. The people of the colony will have a great time making him feel welcome. The Supreme Colony Boss was back there also. This time she'll have to work her way back to the top even harder. Harold and Hugo are dead and buried. And his favorite pastime, ragging on Bennet. He limped through the front door of his apartment and set his keys down on a new glass coffee table. He showered and sat down to watch TV. Nothing of interest was on while he channel surfed so he decided to read a bit. When that lost its novelty, he decided to make something to eat. When he returned from the kitchen however, there was someone waiting for him. Ricky. And he was armed.

"Any last requests?" Ricky asked, as he aimed at David.

"Just one," David said, and moved to his wardrobe, took down the memory box, picked up his mother's kaleidoscope, walked to his window and looked out. New London looked beautiful in the twilight. The neon lights of New Soho were already shining, he could see it from his window. They were that bright. He looked through the kaleidoscope and saw beautiful colours. Blue, red, gold, silver, green, dancing as he spun the tube. Then he heard a gunshot and all the colours turned red, then blurred into nothingness.

Ricky walked over to the wall safe. He tried for a while to guess the code but when that failed he simply shot the lock and it opened. Twenty five thousand credits glowed at him from inside the safe. He took the money and left, slamming the door behind him.

THE END